Career Criminal
III

By: Red Austin

Red Austin

All Rights Reserved.
Copyright © 2021: Keith Austin
1st Print 4/21

This novel is a work of fiction, any resemblance to real people, living or dead, actual events, establishments, organizations, or locales are intended to give the fiction a sense of reality and authenticity. Other names of characters, places, and incidents are either products of the author's imagination or are used fictitiously. Those fictionalized events and incidents that include real persons DID NOT OCCUR and may not be used as if it did.

No part of this work may be reproduced or transmitted in any form or by any means without the written permission from the author.

ISBN: 9798736152360

Contact Information:
KBA Publications
P.O. Box 2863
Phenix City, AL 36868

Chapter 1

Crystal and D.B. were each other's first love-- they both escaped virginity together. Once Crystal's father learned of their relationship, he immediately threatened to send Crystal to live with his mother in Chicago. He disapproved of his daughter dating a thug. Her father was looking out for Crystal's best interest and he needed her to focus more on her education. He wanted her to look toward the future and not live for the moment. He asked Crystal, "what the good girls saw in the bad guys?' She couldn't produce an answer that satisfied his curiosity.

Now that everything that was happening in the dark was coming to the light, seven minutes ago, Crystal gave birth to a healthy 8lb son. The infant was a spitting image of D.B., so she named her child after his father.

As she lay in the hospital bed and held D.B. Jr., she dozed off and revisited the very last time she had made passionate love to D.B. At 2 a.m., her phone rang: "Hello?" she answered, coming out of a deep sleep.

"What's poppin', Rida?", the deep voice bellowed in the base of her phone.

Crystal glanced at the clock on her nightstand.

"Boy, it's 2 o'clock in the morning. Why are you calling me this time of the morning?", she asked, already knowing the answer before she even asked.

"Cause, I'm sitting in front of your house."

"Boy…" she exhaled. "Give me a couple minutes."

Ten minutes later, she was walking across her parent's front lawn with her leather tote bag and velour backpack. Crystal placed her belongings on the backseat and slowly opened the door to the front passenger seat, sliding comfortably into the grooves of the deep leather seat of the Cutlass Supreme, the smell of his air freshener, Black Ice--its masculine scent slowly caressing her nose.

"You are taking me to school in the morning and you better not have me late either," Crystal demanded, making it perfectly clear that she was going to be in her front row desk for attendance later that morning.

"Rida, that's the last thing in the world that I'll try to do is stray you away from your education. I'm just going to be your professor and enhance your knowledge concerning the birds and the bees." D.B. promised, while putting fire to a blunt

"You gonna be my teacher, baby?" Crystal asked in a sultry voice, her eyes slowly taking each inch of D.B. inside her minds' eye. His umber skin shone in the midnight light; she was able to see his prominent nose and supple lips smiling at her--his cheekbones rising to accept her beauty as well.

Crystal's nipples erected and her pussy became soaking wet. She wanted to devour D.B., unzipping his Levi jeans, uncovering the prize withheld by the pristine white Calvin Klein. She wanted to take him into her mouth, all of him, each inch of him until she could not breathe any longer. She wanted to remember the sweet taste of him upon her tongue; she wanted to swallow him whole--the last of his nectar as a prize well-deserved.

D.B.'s full lips always turned her on and he was always ready to explore her soft, sweet pussy. D.B. was so sexy to

Crystal. Her parents had continuously claimed D.B. to be her forbidden fruit-- but to Crystal, he was simply exotic fruit, an unadulterated taste, not for all to consume in one drop just as she had long ago.

"Rida?"

"Yes, love?"

"Tonight, I need all three holes."

Crystal paused and procrastinated. She wanted to decline, but shrieked, all while smiling widely, "You're an animal!"

"This morning, Rida, I'll make you an animal."

"Mmmm…" Crystal moaned as she continued to give D.B. the look that said to him: 'I'm going to fuck your brains out!'

When they arrived at the red light along the dimly lit street, Crystal leaned over and gave D.B. a sopping tongue kiss that immediately made his dick harder than ever; the veins pronounced and excited for her warmth. As they kissed, she tasted the remnants of the weed that coated his sweet, wet tongue. The entire act orgasmic--she moaned once and then again. They stopped once the car behind them beeped their horn, the sharp noise snapping them back to reality.

D.B. passed her the blunt, "Baby girl, put some of this loud pack in your system. It'll help motivate you to throw back that donkey and monkey."

"I'm not a dead fuck," Crystal reminded D.B. as she took another long pull off the blunt.

"I didn't say that" D.B. said as he slowed to turn into the motel. "I just need you to let all of that monkey and donkey out of the cage. I need for us to fuck like two animals. I need to unload my system, release all of this nut, apply pressure," D.B. explained as he precum on himself.

Crystal wanted to ask him why he didn't go home to his wife but decided not to mention Nifitinma; she didn't want to ruin their good spirit.

Crystal loved D.B. and knew he loved her and to her, that was all that mattered in this time and space. As soon as they walked into the room, Crystal wasted no time attacking D.B.'s zipper.

She refused to allow him to get completely naked, she was craving his thickness in her mouth - she had no time to waste. Crystal needed to taste D.B.'s dick. As she yanked his pants down, she began to deep throat D.B.'s his thickness filling her mouth, first fast and then much more slow and deliberate--she wanted to milk him dry. Crystal promised herself that she'll be the best damn headhunter. Usually, she did not want to swallow his cum because she thought it was nasty; but tonight, she wanted to catch the cum with her mouth, not wanting to waste a drop of his juicy love and she refused to allow him to feel cheated. Crystal wanted D.B. to be satisfied and make it hard for Nifitinma or any other female to even compete in the category of headhunter. Her technique was one-of-a-kind, and nothing D. B. had ever experienced.

Crystal ran her tongue up and down the full length of D.B.'s dick, licking from the tip of the mushroom down to his pulsating balls. Her tongue action began to drive him crazy, "Stop teasing me," he managed to say in between his moans and her wet slob that drenched his dick. She made the head disappear into her mouth, licking especially where the pressure had built most. D.B. began to moan even louder and began, slowly, to fuck her mouth as if it was her softness her truly craved. As he thrusted, they both looked into one another's eyes. Crystal's pretty mouth slid up and down and D.B.'s nuts began to hurt because he wanted to cum so badly. As he took one of Crystal's erect nipples between his fingers and began to fondle it, flicking it until it became harder and harder, Crystal began to suck harder and faster. As she let out a cry of ecstasy, as her pussy became even more moist, her clit quavering underneath her panties. She sucked at him hungrily and continued to moan, surprised at her increasing excitement, maybe even more than him, the thought of knowing he was going to cum because of her, seemed to wet the seat of her black lace even more. D.B. pumped away at her mouth. Crystal placed the palm of her hands on the side of his hips to control the pace and force she would suck his dick. She wanted to make sure he didn't thrust his chocolate manhood too hard and fast. This wasn't the time gag or choke. This was the time to secure her man.

Once D.B.'s knees buckled, she knew he was ready to explode, Crystal sucked faster, embracing herself for the rush of salty acridness that awaited her throat.

"Oh shit!!!" D.B. cried out, as he released his bodily fluids into her gaping mouth. She seemed to enjoy his juices gathering about her mouth. She wiped the last remnants off her chin and licked her finger. He gazed at her, not knowing fact from fiction. He groaned and said, "Damn, girl, I love you. Now get naked and lay on the bed."

Upon his command, they both raced to take off the remainder of their clothes. Crystal slid down the nylon shorts she had chosen for their midnight ride, her panties coming down with them. She then laid seductively across the bed as an invitation for D.B. to slide between her thighs.

"Damn these pussy lips beautiful," he confessed, while parting her honey pot with his thumb and pointer finger. He gazed at the soft pink pillow between his fingers and used his tongue to gently suck and kiss her clit. He began to flicker his thick tongue against her pulsating pearl. Crystal moaned in ecstasy, arching her back, driving her pussy in his face with each lick and suck. D.B. could have climaxed again from just the sight of pleasuring his young girl. His tongue pressed inside her, pressing the magic button, his sucking intense yet soft, her wetness filling his mouth. She grabbed at his head, attempting to hold his ears just so she could steady herself to release the stream that rushed from her. After each orgasm, she became less and less able to control her knees shaking. She begged him to stop. He did not, could not. D.B. pushed both of her knees back to her chest aiming his tongue to go deeply inside her opening, sliding all the way down to her butthole. He wanted to taste all of her; he wanted her to know he loved the taste of her.

Crystal cried out with intense pleasure. The first thought to come to her mind was that D.B. was so nasty, but the feeling was so damn good, that it made her love him even more. The tip of D.B.'s tongue touched the g-spot in her ass, causing her pussy to immediately orgasm. Crystal couldn't take the tongue action anymore and began begging for the dick. Her pussy was throbbing and needed to feel all of him.

"Come on baby, fuck me! Fuck this pussy!" she exclaimed, needing to be fucked right now. No more foreplay. No more waiting. She was about to explode at the thought of having to wait another moment for him to throb inside of her juicy walls.

D.B. knew Crystal was waiting to get fucked. But he had to

make her wait, to remind her this is his pussy. As he leaned up to place her in the perfect position for penetration, he saw her sweet pussy smiling at him. The temptation was too strong for D.B. to resist, he had to get another taste of Crystal's sweet and juicy pussy. He gave her large clit a deep long passionate tongue kiss as if he were trying to make love to it. As she began to pour again, he kissed it once again, as if he was simply apologizing for the pain he was about to cause her. In his mind, what was pleasure without pain. He knew she wanted to be rough, but he would make her feel like the woman she was.

"Oh D.B., I love you," she mumbled. "Nigga you said you wanted this pussy, now get it." She mouthed the words fuck me as she licked the edge of his beard that was still soaking from her last squirt. She adjusted herself upon the pillow so that he could enter her. As he found her place and slid deeply inside, she licked the remainder of her pussy juices from his lips. D.B. rammed his dick in and out of her manicured pussy, making her pussy talk to him, uttering phrases only he and her knew.

"Oh, oh, oh," she uttered because D.B. had sucked her pussy until it was too tender to touch. Now it was his turn to give her his joy and pain, "My pussy sore baby."

"Imma beat the soreness out," D.B. promised.

Crystal's pussy became sloppy wet and D.B. continued drilling her. Crystal always made the moaning sound 'mmmh' when she was cumming, so after hearing the 'mmmh' a couple more times, D.B. changed positions. He now wanted her to place both of her legs on his shoulders as he continued to punish her. He beat up in her guts so long, hard, and strong. Crystal matched pound for pound; she was very eager not to be out done. She loved each and every minute of the punishment, in fact. she welcomed it.

"Now I got something else to introduce you to."

"Why?" Crystal asked with lust still in her eyes and voice.

D.B. replaced her legs on his thighs, his dick was well lubricated from their cum. He placed the head of his dick to the mouth of her asshole, "D.B., what are you doing?" she asked, sitting up on her elbows. Crystal was afraid because she never experienced this type of play. She heard so much about it and the fear of the experience was fighting her, "D.B., we never did this before."

"I saw it on a porno flick," D.B. revealed as he continued to work his dick into her. "Now we gotta have sex like porn stars."

"D.B., I'm scared."

"Scared of what?"

"I've never done this before."

"Me neither," D.B. said as he watched his dick head slowly but surely sink into the mouth of Crystal's asshole, "Relax, baby, relax."

Crystal would always speak against having sex in the butt, until her personal trainer told her that it was a beautiful demonstration. Especially when you were doing it with the right person. She told her not to knock it until she tried it.

D.B.'s dick was feeling so damn good at this moment, she wanted to pull it out of her and suck on it, "Ohh, that feels good D.B.." D.B. continued taking his sweet time allowing her muscles to stretch and get use to his love muscle. Crystal peeled back the lips of her pussy, giving D.B. a president's view as she began to push, shove, and force his dick deeper and deeper.

"More, more baby', Crystal moaned. "D.B. please fuck me. You said you was going to turn me into an animal!!"

"You a what?" D.B. asked while wiping sweat from his forehead, "Damn baby you good and tight."

"I-I-I, you're an animal!" Crystal managed to breathe out as the orgasm she was having took complete control over her body. She looked so damn beautiful as she was getting off, that it caused D.B. to unload his nut sack. Afterwards, he hammered home on her kitty-cat until the sun came up. Crystal went to school that morning walking bow legged.

***

After the doctor finished delivering D.B. Jr. into the world, he made his most important phone call of the day: "Mr. Williams, Congratulations! It's a boy!"

On the other end of the receiver, Uncle Louta smiled and replied, "God knew I needed another son."

"And sir, the young lady named the baby just as you expected," the doctor continued, "…the child's named after his father. Yes sir, Mr. Williams, the infant has your last name."

"Good, very good."

The doctor could hear the tension in Uncle Louta's voice and wanted to end the thick phone conversation as quickly as possible, "Sir, is there anything else I can do to accommodate you?" he asked with a shaky and uneasy voice.

"Yes, there is one more thing doc."

"Anything sir, please just name it."

Everyone knew Uncle Louta gave helluva ultimatums and demands. You either do what he says, or he'll threaten to kill you. Even if you thought he wouldn't dare carry out his promise, Uncle Louta would make an example by killing their mate or other family members. However, if you agree out the gate and he'll reward you with money.

"Let's tell the young lady the baby died so I can raise him as my own."

"Fake the child's death?" the doctor questioned.

"Yes."

"Why?"

"Because I need to raise my young generation. I need to put an invisible leash around their necks at a young age. I have to tame, to guide, and most of all, to train them. See, doc, our Williams bloodline is too powerful for their young minds. They do not know or understand the power they possess; I cannot allow my blood to be wasted and to be real with you Doc, this is a Williams thing, your ass could never understand." Uncle Louta finished his request and gave the Doc time to reply. He knew he was pushing his luck with the Doc, but he didn't care. Everyone knew not to fuck with him.

The doctor already knew he couldn't refuse or dismiss Uncle Louta's wishes unless he wanted an early involuntary retirement. He was trying to think of a response in a hurry - too much hesitation was the same as saying no to Uncle Louta.

Uncle Louta was trying to force his hand - maybe he could outthink him and plead on his patient's behalf. "Louta…", he stammered out his first name, trying to hide the uncertainty and overt fear this man was bringing out of him. His hands were shaking, and his forehead was covered with sweat. He knew if he said the wrong thing or showed any disrespect, his body would never be found.

"With all due respect sir, I have never ever disobeyed not one of your orders, not one. But it so happens that the young lady's father is a very dear friend of mine. This young lady loves her child so much already. Plus, the child is all she has left of the father. Louta I beg you please don't make me do this," the doctor pleaded with tears in his eyes. He had done the unthinkable- he questioned Uncle Louta. He bit down on his knuckle and silently thought, *Dear God, for once please allow this devil to have a heart.'*

Uncle Louta exhaled. His breath created a cold hard blanket over the phone receiver. "Alright, doc." He paused again, taking his time to speak each of his words clearly and slowly. He did this deliberately. He wanted Doc to know this was his shit and his call. He was the motherfucking boss - not him. He wasn't taking no fucking orders from a nigga off the street so he for damn sure wasn't stut'n shit this square ass nigga was talking about.

Instead of clapping on his ass, he stopped. He decided to create leverage. "Imma do you this one solid - just this one. Imma give your scary ass a pass. Imma allow this little girl and her father to keep the child. But Doc……"

"Yes, Mr. Williams?" Doc replied, relieved but even more fearful of what was to come next.

Uncle Louta heard the shaking in the Doc's voice. He thought to himself, he was so easy to fucking scare, let me chill before I have his clown ass shitting on himself. He quickly changed his tone from gangsta to professional, "I'm going to keep a close eye on this family and that child. Doc, I'll sleep with one eye open."

"Yes sir, I understand. I thank you for considering my please. May God Bless you!" Doc was so happy he was off Louta's radar that he was crying tears of joy and giving God silent praises.

"Doc, I don't know how in the hell that I allowed you to sweet talk me out of going against my own will. But let me make some shit clear." Louta's professionalism went out the window, he heard too much relief in Doc's voice and knew he needed to shake him up- remind him he don't show mercy without a price. "I know this is the righteous thing to do. I know what's best for my people. I know what they need before they even know that they need. They don't need too much freedom from the start. They have to be properly instructed at a young age, because if not, there will be no room for a leash to be placed around their neck once they get a taste, smell, or sight of blood. They have the same blood running through their veins as I have in mine - and we are all fucking savages. I better not regret my decision, or it's your head I am coming for!"

Uncle Louta slammed the receiver down. He was unsettled about the decision he made and knew it was a bad idea. He silently asked himself, ``*Am I getting too old for this shit or am*

I becoming soft? When did I start letting a motherfucker suggest shit to me and keep his tongue?!

As he was pondering the decision he just made, his wife Deyarna, came to him and began to rub his back. She knew something was vexing her love, but she never pried or hounded him for information - she just allowed him to be. What she needed to know he would tell her when the time was right. Until then, she played her most important role - she took care of her King.

"Is everything ok King?" She already knew it wasn't, she asked more out of courtesy. She knew she wasn't going to receive the truth. "Would you like me to make you some coffee? Are you ready to go back to bed?"

Deyarna wished she could've got out of bed and answered the phone instead of her King. But Uncle Louta explained to her, never to answer that phone - the only time the phone was for business and she didn't need to know.

"I'm going back to bed, but I need to check on my sons," Uncle Louta told her as he walked into the bedroom where seven year old Keisword Jr., his four year old baby brother Keiwon, and their other five year old brother Keiray slept.

The first two boys came from Thy and the five-year-old came from Kawaii, both of Keisword's baby mamas were young, struggling, and catching extreme hell trying to make ends meet. One dropped out of college, the other one didn't finish high school because she was pregnant. They allowed Keisword to fuck them as he pleased. He rightly obliged to their request but added his own special flare- babies.

Kawaii's mother's mother told her that education came first, and dick came last, but she wouldn't listen. Thy's mother just didn't give a fuck - she had her own shit going on to worry about.

Keisword took good care of his kids and truly loved their mother. In a perfect world, he would have been with both of them at the same time. But the world isn't perfect, and he wasn't either.

Four months after Keisword's death, Uncle Louta grew tired of watching PK give both baby mothers the moral support that was needed. Uncle Louta wanted more for the young ladies than what they wanted for themselves. So, he gave them a deal they couldn't refuse. Uncle Louta offered to give them each a quarter of a million dollars if they gave him Keisword's children because. He wanted to personally raise the boys, to keep them together, and most of all, keep them close to Keisword's mother, who was Uncle Louta's baby sister. Kawaii and Thy could keep their children on the weekends and holidays, but by paper Uncle Louta and his wife Deyarna were the legal guardians. They adopted the babies.

Thy and Kawaii came around as they pleased, they were family. Actually, Uncle Louta loved when they came around. Several times, the boys inquired about their mothers, they would ask Uncle Louta questions like, "Does their mother love them? Why don't their mother's come and pick them up? Why can't they live with their mothers?"

These questions caused Uncle Louta to renegotiate the contracts he made with their mothers. Instead of coming and going as they please - Thy and Kawaii had to buy them presents, pick them up from school, cook them dinner and spend weekends and holidays all under Uncle Louta's roof. Uncle Louta always made sure that the young ladies left with a handsome reward since he had it to throw and blow. He did not care about the money, he just wanted to ensure the kids knew they were loved. The two women weren't just babymommas, they were all a functioning family.

Uncle Louta smiled; it melted the old die hard Triple OG heart to see his great-nephews sleeping in peace. He loved them boys as if they were his own. Keeping the bloodline together was something that he vowed to do- he wouldn't let anyone get in the way of his goal.

Deyarna was also glad to have the children. They brought more life to Uncle Louta, made him softer - the man she fell in love with. She loved to watch him spend quality time with them and cook for them. They called Uncle Louta daddy. Deyarna smiled and daydreamed about the last time Louta asked the kids about life.

"Keisword, what you going to be when you grow up?" Louta asked as his brother Keiwon jumped from his lap to pick up a bright red firetruck lying on the floor near them.

"Imma go in the service like you, Daddy. Daddy imma fly great big 'ole planes like you."

"Keiray, what you going to be?"

"Imma drive the ambulance daddy." He took pride in saying the word because for the longest time he said ambelance. His mother and Deyarna told him that if that's what he wanted to be, he needed to pronounce the word correctly. He practiced for days and when he finally said it right, he was so proud that he practically yelled the word wherever he went. Keiray was enthusiastic and passionate about his dream. He would talk about driving ambulances from sunrise until sunset and ask anyone who would listen a

million questions.

"Keiwon?"

"Huh?"

"What you going to be son?"

Keiwon was in the midst of pushing around his fire truck, *"Imma drive this truck."*

Keisword Jr. raced over to his baby brother and whispered into his ear and Keiwon shouted loud and proud, "Imma fire fighter!"

Deyarna abandoned the old days and snapped out of her daydream. Simplistic family time was a thing of the past as of lately. Everything has just been business, business, business. She knew something was troubling her King, but he hasn't shared it yet. *He will when he is ready*, she thought to herself.

She found Louta looking over the boys and watched him silently for a few moments before breaking his trance. "Come on baby, let's go back to bed before you mess around and wake up the children and you know they gonna want to play," she said gently while taking his hand to lead him out of the room.

Uncle Louta carefully closed the bedroom door, "Yeah, you right Sweetheart, I better not awaken the beasts." He laughed, "…because if I did that, I wouldn't be able to get me no milk and cookies."

"Oh really? I have some cookies hot out of the oven just for you. Louta, I thought I was going to have to wake you up and steal the dick." Deyarna confessed. She knew Louta was a light sleeper. Normally, she could get in and out of bed a few times to wake him up and he would be ready to blow her mind. She needed to feel his manhood tonight. She got in and out of the bed countless times trying to throw a hint. She needed to relieve some stress - but he wouldn't wake up. Even after gently kissing his neck and whispering "wake up…. kitty needs you." He did not budge. That is how she knew something was weighing on him. She knew what was wrong, he was dreaming of Gangsta Slim, Risgo, and the girls. Once he started thinking about them, nothing could snap him out of his thoughts….no even Pretty Kitty.

"You was going to wake me up baby?" Uncle Louta asked in a sexy voice. He knew what she had been trying to do all night. His mind was just on business shit and he wasn't in the mood. He knew he was wrong though. His wife was loyal and did not ask for much - the least he could do was satisfy her fine ass. She has always been loyal and selfless, his bottom bitch since he met her.

"When a woman needs to be loved by her sexy husband, she won't sleep right, she will be restless." she moaned softly while flicking her tongue back and forth slowly on his earlobe.

"I'm sorry baby," Uncle Louta said while moving her face from his ear. She stared at him - hungrily, anxious, her eyes pleading for him to make her pussy cream. He leaned in closely to her, inhaling her CoCo Chanel perfume and gently used his hands to part her legs. He kissed her deep and long while moving his index finger and thumb across her throbbing clit. She moaned with delight - he placed his pussy soaked fingers in her mouth and commanded her to lick them clean. After she finished tasting herself, he told her to get her ass in the bedroom and put on something sexy.

After all these years, Deyarna was the only woman to ever have Louta pussywhipped. He loved her more than anything in this world - himself included. It is a good thing Deyarna coaxed him into sex that night because he was on the way to pay the doctor an unannounced house call. He wanted to kill that motherfucker for making him change his mind. He was disobedient and he had to die. He knew what he wanted. Why in the fuck did he let him talk out taking the baby?

Deryarna waited for Louta for fifteen minutes and he still did not come to the bedroom. This was not like him at all and she knew something was really wrong. She found him in his study sipping a glass of cognac in heavy thought.

"Louta," she called his name quietly, trying to select her words carefully. She did not want to upset him anymore than he already was.

"Yes, dear?"

"When you sleep hard, that's when you have something heavy on your mind. Am I right?"

"Yes, Sweetheart."

"Louta, what you stressing about?"

"About my family... About them Ridaz..."

"I need you here with me at this very moment. Louta, I need you to be my Rida. So, are you ready to ride? Can you ride, Rida?"

"I'm not too old to ride you, Rida."

Deyarna was a young stallion, she was big-boned, and cornbread fed, plus she had an extremely healthy appetite for sex.

Uncle Louta laid back on the couch. He dick was at attention as he watched her drop the black silk robe to the ground. He licked his lips as her nipples hardened from the touch of cool air. She did not waste any time straddling his hardness, her pussy was still creamy from the finger fuck before. He gripped the sides of her plump peach and everything worrying him melted away. He used his strong hands to make her pump forward, faster, and faster until he felt her waterfall explode all over his dick.

"Oh, oh, oh… Yes baby… Mmmmhh…" she cooed.

"Ride it, Rida" he grunted as she took him to ecstasy.

***

CHAPTER 2

Detective Narma fastened the buttons on his long sleeve white shirt. Today was one of the most important days of his life. His family, Pete's family, and Reese's family are looking forward to this special day. These three men are being sworn in as F.B.I. agents. Narma, Reese, and Pete celebrated all last night and none of them slept well. They were too excited.

"Dear, are you ready for me to tie your tie?" Detective Narma's wife, Connie asked after she slipped into her black Louboutins.

"Sure dear, why not," Detective Narma said.

Once Connie slipped the black tie around his neck, she pulled him to her and gave him a kiss on the lips, "I'm proud of you, husband."

"Personally, I think they should have been promoted me," Detective Narma grinned at his beautiful wife, "What do you think Sweetheart?"

"I agree," his wife replied as she continued to fix his tie.

"I'm glad Reese and Pete got the promotion as well. My partners bust their butts on these cases right along with me."

"I'm happy for them as well," Connie said. She was still struggling with getting his tie just right.

"You think we'll make good F.B.I. agents?"

"Of course, dear. How could you great guys not?" She finally got the size of the knot correct.

Beep-beep-beep–beeeep-beep!! A car horn blew outside.

Detective Narma looked out of his bedroom window. Detective Reese and his mother were parked in front of his house. Detective Reese was waving to him as a sign that meant, *come on, let's go.* He held his watch up and pointed at it, hoping Detective Narma could see his gestures through his windshield window.

This caused Narma to look at his own wristwatch and he noticed he was running a little behind.

"Alright, I see I'm running a little late. I'm on my way." Detective Narma said, even though he knew Detective Reese, nor his mother could hear what he was saying. He threw both of his hands up over his head trying to gesture to them he was sorry.

"Honey, are we running late," asked his wife, she was finishing up his tie,

"Yes, Sweetheart," Detective Narma answered, "Reese and his mother are outside waiting, c'mon, we gotta go."

"Let's not keep them waiting," Connie said. Even though she had been ready twenty-one minutes ago. "Narma, we don't need to keep them sitting out there in the car with it being as hot as it is. Reese's mother is too old to have to fight the heat on our account."

"I'm ready, Sweetheart. I don't want her to have a heat stroke," he joked as he grabbed his jacket and headed to the front door.

When Narma and Connie finally walked out their door, Detective Pete and his family were parked behind Detective Reese. It looked as if they were lining up for a funeral caravan. Narma and Connie waived to both families before getting into their vehicle. Thanks to Narma, they all will be late on their big day.

Detective Narma, Reese, and Pete spent 16 weeks training

in Virginia at Quantico. During their graduation, everyone was given an envelope. Inside the envelope was a color; red meant that one operation would be interesting. Green meant two operations would be interesting and yellow meant that several operations that would be interesting.

Narma received green in his envelope. Reese and Pete's envelope revealed the color red. Since counter-terrorism operations were interesting to all three of them, they decided to accept that field so they all would be together. Besides, they specialized in and had a passion for chasing bad guys.

After their boss, Agent Coin finished welcoming them into the bureau, the three agents had their private get together once again to celebrate. Narma and Pete drank small shots of liquor, Reese had cherry 7up in his glass.

"I would like to make a toast to us retiring together," Reese announced and held up his glass to make a toast.

"I would like to make a toast to our year probation with the bureau," Pete said as they all clinked their glasses together.

Narma gave his piece as the glasses clinked from the toasting, "Reese and Pete, both of you guys are my brothers. Remember the measurement and quality of a brother's love is governed by a long-term interest bearing an endless bond."

They all drank their glasses and exchanged congratulations. The mood was set. Everyone was relaxing and daydreaming about their future successes and what their new roles will entail.

Reese was the first to open the old wounds and break the silence, "What you guys think about the Williams boys?"

"Career Criminals!!!" Pete said angrily slamming his glass down on the table.

"You meant to say the Career Criminals and Ridaz?" Narma corrected taking a deep gulp from his glass.

Just the mention of the Career Criminals and Ridaz was enough to shift the entire mood of the room. Reese, Narma, and Pete all hated the crew and their malicious ways and would do whatever they needed to see them behind bars for the rest of their lives.

"Yes, what's you guys take on them?" Reese asked, already knowing everyone's response.

"This conversation here calls for a cigar!" Pete said as he pulled the half smoked and half chewed cigar from his shirt pocket. Any conversation called for a cigar, Pete just loved to smoke, and his brothers all hated the smell.

"All hell!," Reese said thinking of the stinky smoke he was about to inhale.

"This a non-smoking area," Narma stated, pointing to the non-smoking sign.

"Thank you, Jesus!!!" Reese exclaimed in relief.

"We're saved by the bell," Narma said laughing.

"Pete, that's one cancer stick we will not have to deal with." Reese said.

"Pete, we don't want to lose you to cancer," Narma said genuinely concerned.

"At least it'll only damage the inside of my body," Pete said with a good sense of humor "...These so-called bad guys throwing bullets. They trying to knock limits off of our bodies."

Reese patted Pete on the back, "Big guy, I agree because cancer is treatable if you catch it in an early stage. I heard second-hand smoke is something serious. They say it'll cause more damage to the individual who is actually doing the smoking." Reese was trying to throw Pete a hint, but he wasn't hearing it at all. Instead, Pete tried to put the cigar in Reese's mouth,

"So, partner, what you trying to say? You ready to start smoking?" Pete struggled to get his words out because he was laughing so hard.

"Not in a million years!" Reese turned his nose up while moving the pungent cigar out of his face. He then began to refill his empty glass with 7up.

Pete noticed Narma had that glare in his eyes, which he had seen and recognized on many occasions, "What's bothering you, Narma?"

"Louta," Narma said in a harsh tone, "and his family! First, it was the guys and now I'll be damn if it ain't the girls. They done joined this crazy-killing death wish."

"The Williams crew will fuck up a wet dream," Reese unconsciously publicized.

"They have no heart, no mercy…" Narma blurted out as if he were hypnotized, "…Louta trained them to show no love unless it's among family. Louta created, molded, and converted his family into cold-hearted killers."

"Demons," Reese said, "would be more like it."

"Knowing them guys and Louta's unlimited resources they are probably traveling all around the world terrorizing shit" Narma predicted.

"I hope to God that you wrong," Reese said giving Narma his undivided attention, "and please for God's sake, let's not speak things into existence."

Reese poured himself a drink of liquor and decided at this

moment it was the best time as ever to take a swig of the strong, stiff drink.

"The world can't hold them because their ambition is extremely strong and they get bigger and better plans as the days, months, and years squeeze on by," Pete said.

CHAPTER 3

Gangsta Slim watched in silence as the snow-white hair and bearded Tycoon drained his double on the rocks glass of liquor. As he finished the last few drops of the cognac-colored liquid, he thought about the past and current situations. Over the last few years, he fed Gangsta Slim and the Ridaz a lick here and there. They would make anywhere from a half to a couple million per mission. Now just as Uncle Louta predicted, his family's patience and consistency finally paid off. Their loyalty no longer needed to be tested any further.

"Son, your Uncle Louta said that you all will be able to handle any and every job I'm able to throw you guys' way." The Tycoon spoke with pride and confidence: "Now I'm able to say I agree with Louta one-hundred percent. I love you guys' work. You get in quick and get the hell out of dodge. I like that", his mouth curling into a smile.

"Thank you, sir." Gangsta Slim said, as he toyed around with his glass of liquor.

He didn't want to ruin the Tycoon celebration by coming clean by admitting he didn't drink. He didn't feel like answering the questions that usually came when he denied a drink, so he accepted and thought it would be in his best interest not to decline.

"I'm glad you're pleased with our assistance sir."

"Son, just as Louta promised, you and your crew have made us plenty of bucks." The Tycoon confessed while refilling his glass with the glass decanter resting on the bar.

"Yes, we have done great business together", Gangsta Slim thought before repeating the words aloud.

"I would've been nothing without you guys." The Tycoon said. Some of the jobs he had tried to give other crews, they would turn them down. There wasn't a mission that Tycoon couldn't meltdown and pour on Gangsta Slim and the Ridaz that they would shake off.

"If there is a will, there is a way" said the Tycoon, laughing as he repeated Gangsta Slim's words because Gangsta Slim always enjoyed finding a way to accommodate his mission. He refused to allow any situation to outsmart him.

"There's always a way." Gangsta Slim stated what Uncle Louta taught him and his cousins at a very, very young age.

"I agree Mr. Thinker," The Tycoon said as he held his glass toward Gangsta Slim as if he were making a toast. After taking a large swallow he began: "Hard work, dedication, motivation, and plenty of orchestration."

"I plan the work and work the plan," Gangsta Slim said truthfully.

"I like that son. Plan your work and work your plan," Tycoon repeated.

Little did he know, Gangsta Slim had always studied him and now he'd seen with his own eyes that the Tycoon had been a lowkey alcoholic equipped with a tender dick. The Tycoon was not only wealthy, powerful, and important, he was also apt to making mistakes, in which a man of his status should be infallible.

He's an old rich fool as well as a very intelligent guy, Gangsta Slim thought as he continued to do as he did best, look, listen, and learn.

"Son, I have given you and your people jobs that my other partners in crime wouldn't dare touch." The Tycoon's intoxicated mind spoke his sober heart, "I even said to my damn self, how in the hell are they going to pull this shit off?

"I'm known for pulling a rabbit out of the hat," Gangsta Slim replied, a serious look coming across his face.

It was very hard to hold his attitude hostage and he had to constantly remind himself what separated him from others. What made him unique was that he was always able to think through a situation instead of fighting the situation with brute force. Uncle Louta always reminded him that the person who did the most thinking will always be the most successful. Besides, Gangsta Slim knew he had to bite his tongue because he needed the Tycoon. He fed them major scores.

"You guys are fearless" the Tycoon reminded Gangsta Slim trying not to slur his words.

"We are Williams, and we have blood lines that are extremely powerful" Gangsta Slim replied. He knew that he had to keep coaxing and reassuring the Tycoon that he was as he appeared: cool and collected.

"Louta is a living witness," The Tycoon states, making it known that he had personally witnessed Uncle Louta's work. He knew deep down that Louta didn't give a flying fuck about nothing and nobody. Louta also refused to allow anything to stand in the way of him getting to the paper, hence the reason why he only hired family. It had been Louta's true purpose of teaching Gangsta Slim so young-- he wanted his family to know what loyalty felt like so they would never forget.

This man was not a fool; he didn't get to where he is now by being a dummy, Gangsta Slim began to think. He remembered that The Tycoon was ambitious, and in the event of him fumbling the ball, he had enough money, material wealth, and common sense to correct any and every last one of his errors. It was only once he'd become careless and this was the wrong time to fumble the ball.

"Slim?"

"Yes sir?"

"I have a serious mission for you and your people," Tycoon said in a serious tone.

Gangsta Slim smiled because he didn't like to talk about his Uncle. Even though the stranger in front of him did know his Uncle before he was born, he was just big on loyalty. He didn't want the Tycoon to slip up and say the wrong thing because there is he has no understanding when it comes to his family.

"Now you're speaking my language," Gangsta Slim said as he continued to smile.

"A billion-dollar lick."

"What's your take?"

"The usual."

"Twenty-five percent?" Gangsta Slim questioned as his eyes sparkled like they always did when The Tycoon started talkin' them digits.

"Why certainly, young man. The lil' bitty twenty-five percent will be just fine for me as always." The Tycoon's face became stone, "I give you guys this mission because I know it can be accomplished. And only you and your people have the capability to pull it off."

"What brings you to that conclusion?"

"Because you all are Williams," The Tycoon stated without a smile because he was serious. "You all were trained by the best and with your thinking ability and expertise, nothing is impossible. The movie 'Mission Impossible' will never have shit on you and your crew."

Gangsta Slim disregarded the compliment, because nothing or no one could talk him into doing anything he didn't want to do. But for some strange reason, he felt obligated to do this job. Since dealing with the Tycoon, Gangsta Slim had learned to enjoy completing the jobs that other criminals feared, and thought couldn't be done. These 'hard' jobs were intriguing, and they gave him a sense of pure rush and a hard-on that his wife called a feeling of pleasure with pain.

"So, what's the job's capital?"

"Nuclear bombs," the Tycoon said. He paused to give Gangsta Slim the opportunity to decline before he gave all of the details.

"Please continue," Gangsta Slim said as he crossed his legs to make his erect penis incognito.

He welcomed any and all challenges. When Gangsta Slim was young, he fought battles knowing they couldn't be won. As he got older, Uncle Louta showed him from first-hand experience that if there was a will, there was a way. He also showed him how not to fight a situation with angry force. But to think a situation through thoroughly, giving each plan meticulous care and ultimate thought. Gangsta Slim always weighed out all of his options. He'd analyze the situation from every possible angle. Then he would break them down, sometimes, he'd re-break them down and turn back around and rebuild them. Uncle Louta's favorite question to ask was: 'You gonna let this little situation outthink you?' In his mind, the reply was always *hell no.* He didn't have your average 'criminal mind'. He didn't always think of the outcome; he had to consider all the risks just in case there is room for error. In his mind, there was no room for errors. His mind was too strong for his body. Gangsta Slim could be thinking about simple things and his mind wouldn't allow him to rest until he mentally solved the situation at least a dozen different ways.

"There are seven nuclear bombs that five scientists are building. They'll be finished with them in about six more months. I can get you and another one of your people amongst the scientists. I'm talking about actually inside the actual room where the nuclear weapons are being created." The Tycoon stated and decided to reward his mouth with the taste of his liquor.

"How would we be able to high-jack the seven missiles?" Gangsta Slim asked.

Now he was becoming even more interested in the job.

"Not the missiles," The Tycoon corrected. "Son, the nuclear warheads are only the size of a football. Shit, you can carry all seven of them lil' shits by yourself."

"Sounds good to me," Gangsta Slim raised a finger, "but how would we be able to get away undetected? Common sense tells me they'll be well guarded."

The Tycoon toyed around with his glass of liquor. He stared into the glass and watched the liquor and small ice cubes square dance around one another, clashing and cascading in the brown pool of motivator.

"Son, that's your problem. My problem is to sell the damn things; to get us a nice buyer who's willing to pay our price and not try to talk us out of our shit."

"Where are the warheads located?"

"North Korea."

"North Korea?" Gangsta Slim exhaled. "...and I don't know shit concerning nuclear warheads."

"I'm pretty sure by the time our six months conclude, you'll fuck around and become a scientist." The Tycoon thought of his own joke and started laughing.

"What makes you so sure?" Gangsta Slim questioned him, wanting to see what type of encouraging, better yet, assuring feedback he would give.

"Seventy-five percent of a billion," The Tycoon laughed again. "Louta tells me that you're a fast learner. Your ability to camouflage is no different than a chameleon's-- whatever you land on will be the color you'll become. And besides, for that type of money, me, and you both would try to be astronauts if we had to! I mean, whatever you and I need to be to get to the paper, that's what we will become.

Gangsta Slim liked the older, generous gentleman, even though he sometimes made comments that made him appear to be an asshole. Somehow, he would count on the Tycoon to always come back and correct himself with something clever.

"Son, you saw the people who were on the lower deck?"

"Yes."

"They will be your tutors and for our sake, when they give you the test to see what you have learned, please do us both a favor by not guessing the answer." The Tycoon put his sailor's captain's hat on and cocked it slightly to the right, "if you don't know the correct answer, say so, and know there's only one dumb question."

"The one you never asked," Gangsta Slim answered.

"Son, you'll be just fine," The Tycoon said. "My people will give you lots of info. I also have the inside connect for you. They'll be beside you 24-7. When you take a shit and piss, they'll guard your door. They'll be your shadows."

"How many scientists will be in there again?"

"Five."

"How would I be able to tie into them?" Gangsta Slim asked, as he uncrossed his legs.

"Always remember this, amongst five scientists, there will always be one amongst the group that will be looked upon as an outcast. The others will probably not take to him for some reason maybe." The Tycoon began to count on his fingers each one of the reasons they probably wouldn't like the other scientist or take to him. "They may not like him because he's smarter than the rest of them put together, or vice-versa. He may be the one who is in charge of them. He might be a party-pooper. Son, if you study them very closely, the one you are looking for will team up with you. It'll be his pleasure to sell out on the others. Probably even be the biggest thrill of his evening and he'll make history. The other scientists are simple ordinary people. I promise you; the son-a-bitch will be one elite muthafucka under the roof." The Tycoon spoke from experience.

"This one helluva challenge," Gangsta Slim confessed.

"To you, son, it's only a sloppy wet piece of pussy, ready to get fucked," the Tycoon said tipping his hat to Gangsta Slim.

The Tycoon laughed inside at his private joke because he

noticed when Gangsta Slim crossed his legs to hide his hard-on.

***

Six Months Later…

Gangsta Slim watched the five scientists with eagle eyes until Yan Kibble began to stick out as though he was a sore thumb. The other scientist hated his guts, because the man was too brilliant for his five-foot four-inch frame. To make matters even worse, his head was too large for his body. One Sunday morning in class, his teacher advised him to use his head for more than a hat rack.

Their school was seven days a week year round; there was no such thing called a break let alone a spring break. Yan Kibble knew the answer before the teachers or instructor could or would finish asking the question. He often got into trouble for shouting out the answer. They also would ask him to give the other students an opportunity to answer the question. Yan Kibble could and would produce the correct answer quicker than a fish could take a bath in water. The other scientist would always have to come to him for answers.

Three months after Gangsta Slim was there, a scientist came back and asked Yan Kibble the same question he previously asked a couple of days ago. And before Yan Kibble could repeat the answer, Gangsta Slim blurted out the answer. Yan Kibble gave him a high-five and stated, "Great minds think alike."

From that day forward, Yan Kibble would al-ways small

talk with Gangsta Slim and to his surprise Yan Kibble would talk down on the other scientist. He would also unconsciously enlighten Gangsta Slim about his private life; basically, he was a loner. He said he never had a friend. No one liked him due to his head being too big for his shoulders, and because he was too intelligent to converse with.

"Mr. Fedish, sir, how are you coming along?" Yan Kibble addressed Gangsta Slim by his name tag.

"Mr. Kibble, thanks to you sir, I can say I worked underneath one of the world's greatest geniuses," Gangsta Slim said, stroking Yan Kibble's ego.

"Geez, no one's ever compared me to a genius before."

"Mr. Kibble, sir, remember there is always a first time for everything." Gangsta- Slim knew exactly what to say to Yan Kibble. He was an easy target to use for information.

"In that case, I must let you in on a big 'ole secret," Yan Kibble said waving Gangsta Slim over so he could bend over and allow him to whisper into his ear. Yan Kibble always did this amongst the other scientist as well as when they were out in the public, "I'm a forty-year old and I never had my first piece of hot sex yet."

"You tryna tell me that you still a virgin?" Gangsta Slim asked whispering back into Yan Kibble's ear. *This is going to be easier than I thought*, Gangsta Slim said to himself. *He never had no ass - oh hell yea, Imma get him some pussy and he is going to tell me everything I need to fucking know.*

"Yes, sir."

One of the scientists cleared his throat loudly, "MMMM, Hmmmn! Excuse me, gentlemen, but it's not polite to whisper."

Yan Kibble began to whistle because today he felt the need to be a wise ass, especially since they would always team up against him. Yan Kibble felt like he finally had an ally, a friend. He wasn't solo anymore.

"Mr. Kibble, I can assist you in that department: I mean, in that field." Gangsta Slim assured him.

"What?" Yan Kibble shouted out as he became excited. He did his little chicken dance, "What-what-what!!" He gave Gangsta Slim a high-five, "...if you can set that up, then you're a genius."

"I know a sweetheart that will make your toes curl and you'll be in another world." Gangsta Slim whispered into Yan Kibble's ear.

"What-what-what!!!!" Yan Kibble began doing the chicken dance once again for the record.

"Mr. Kibble, sir, have you heard of a genie being in a lamp?"

"No, sir."

"Well, I'm your genie in the lamp, I'll grant three of your wishes."

"Mr. Fedish, sir, I already told you my wish."

"Mr. Kibble, consider your wish granted."

Gangsta Slim knew where to go to solve Yan Kibble's problem and to bring about solving the situation would be music to his dear friend the Tycoon's ears.

The Tycoon had two yachts; one for when he wanted to be alone or needed privacy; the other one he kept docked and filled with beautiful and exotic women from all around the globe. There was a helicopter on both yachts and the Tycoon had models flown in and out. They revolved around his schedule. Gangsta Slim asked the Tycoon why one of his yachts stayed filled with women? The Tycoon explained he spent a decade straight behind bars and he didn't want to wait until he died to see angels. Plus, since he spent the golden years of his life with hard legs, he now wanted to spend the rest of his life in heaven. To the Tycoon, heaven was between some legs and being caked up wit' that bread.

Gangsta Slim became the brother that Yan Kibble never knew could've existed. He took Yan Kibble to the yacht and converted him into a cold-blooded stud. Yan Kibble began to think with his little head more than his big bead. The Adidas sign was invisibly stamped on his forehead: *all day I dream about sex.* Yan Kibble and Gangsta Slim had something in common, they both were addicted to fucking.

It's a damn shame that when the time comes, I'm gonna have to murder Mr. Kibble, Gangsta Slim thought as he watched Yan Kibble write some information down on a notepad.

"What's on your mind?" Yan Kibble asked, he could tell his new brother was thinking about something, "S-E-X..." Gangsta Slim lied.

"And me too..." Yan Kibble honestly agreed.

***

The day the nuclear warheads were completed, Gangsta Slim finally came to his senses. He realized that this mission was more difficult in more ways than one. He didn't have the first clue as to how to handle the war heads with care. Secondly, if something were to go wrong during the transport of these nuclear weapons, he would be putting his loved ones in harm's way. He reasoned with himself day in and day out. Gangsta Slim was faced with a very, very hard dilemma. He wouldn't be successful without Yan Kibble's assistance because Yan Kibble knew the ins and outs of the missiles. Yan Kibble had the qualifications to be the babysitter. Now, Gangsta Slim was forced to put his trust into a stranger. He had to open up to Yan Kibble and come clean by confessing that he was out to steal the nuclear warheads. If Yan Kibble was intelligent as Gangsta Slim and the other scientist gave him credit for, then Yan Kibble wouldn't hesitate nor procrastinate about getting on the winning team. Now, on the other hand, Gangsta Slim hoped like hell that Yan Kibble wouldn't commit suicide and blow the whole place sky high out of fear.

"Mr. Kibble, I have something serious that I need to discuss with you," Gangsta Slim said.

He was ready to kill Yan Kibble if he didn't cooperate.

"I'm listening… I'm a very good listener."

"I don't know no other way to say this but to be straight forward," Gangsta Slim said.

Yan Kibble's eyes rambled around his one-bedroom, cheap apartment taking in the sight of his cheap furniture. His mind and intuition let him know this was a serious matter- maybe even life or death. Mr. Kibble hoped that for the first time in his life, he was wrong about a prediction and the forthcoming conversation would be simple and easy.

"Mr. Kibble, I'm here to steal the nuclear war heads. And I'll---…"

Yan Kibble immediately volunteered, "I'll assist you in any and every way possible. Please I beg you just don't kill me. I can be of a great assistance to you."

Gangsta Slim could hear the sincerity in the little guy's voice and see the fear in his eyes. Gangsta Slim went against his will, against everything he stood for, and against his principles and foundation. His top-priority was to kill all five of the scientists, not sparing Yan Kibble in the least.

"Mr. Fetish…" Yan Kibble began speaking for his life and for his freedom, "You'll need me, because if these warheads are not properly handled, then you'll mess around and blow up the whole planet!"

"That's what I'm afraid of," Gangsta Slim admitted to his fear.

The problem came in because he had put the Ridaz and Risgo's life in danger. Why gamble with their life when he had the fat-head stranger?

"I can convert this thing into a two-man job," Gangsta Slim was thinking until Yan Kibble killed his concentration.

"Mr. Fedish, if you would do me one favor and I'll do the rest, I'll make your job easier than you ever thought it would be."

"What's your favor?"

"Execute my other four co-workers."

"Consider it done," Gangsta Slim said rubbing his palms together.

"Mr. Fedish?"

"Yes."

"It would be a pleasure to assist you, sir."

Gangsta Slim broke his plan down; he explained everything to Yan Kibble. Yan Kibble digested the idea; he meditated long and hard. Gangsta Slim respected his silence and when Yan Kibble's mouth did fly back open, he had agreed. Gangsta Slim was astonished, because Yan Kibble's best asset was that big-ass turd that sat on his shoulders.

"Two heads are better than one," Gangsta Slim said.

"People used to call me two heads when I was a child," Yan Kibble said as if he unloaded a great deal of burdens.

Yan Kibble always stated facts; he didn't talk just because he had a mouth or because he wanted to exercise his tongue. The more and more they talked, the more comfortable they became with one another. From time to time, Gangsta Slim would revisit their plan just to make sure there wasn't something that Yan Kibble needed to make him aware of but probably forgot to tell him. But as it turns out that wasn't the case because Yan Kibble actually acted out the entire plan in his head several times before he shared them with Gangsta Slim. Yan Kibble even murdered the other four scientists himself, but he failed to share that part.

Bright and early the next morning, everything unfolded according to plan. Gangsta Slim killed the other scientists. Him and Yan Kibble were able to walk scot-free off the premises with the seven nuclear warheads. Yan Kibble and Gangsta Slim boarded the private jet; Keisword Jr and Uncle Louta were their pilot and co-pilot.

"Well, well, well. What do we have here?" A beautiful stewardess said upon serving Gangsta Slim and Yan Kibble. She thought for a split-second Yan Kibble was something that came out of the circus or out of an alien movie.

"What, what, what!!!" Yan Kibble shouted, doing his famous chicken dance; Gangsta Slim knew the small guy was excited.

"Please meet the genius himself, live in the flesh and

blood…" Gangsta Slim said smiling as he introduced Yan Kibble "...but he's also known as 'The Brain' or the 'Architect'."

"Oh okay," the stewardess said knowing Yan Kibble carried some type of importance.

"G, she's hot, hot, hot…" Yan Kibble said, blowing into both of his small palms, "...babe's a game-changer. Now I'm officially throwing in my player's cards."

Gangsta Slim told Yan Kibble he was a genius; Yan Kibble repeated the same sentence verbally back to Gangsta Slim. Once Gangsta Slim explained everything to Uncle Louta, Uncle Louta gave Yan Kibble the nickname Architect. Uncle Louta told Gangsta Slim that he did the rightful thing by trusting the stranger and by having the Ridaz and Risgo's best interests at heart.

"Son, I always trusted your judgement."

"Big Chief, I always try to think like you."

Uncle Louta smiled, "What for? When you're the true mastermind, and with Yan Kibble by your side you'll be much more successful."

"He's a genius," Gangsta Slim stated.

"And also, a great architect," Uncle Louta added with a smile.

CHAPTER 4

13 Years Later...

D.B.'s mother and Keisword's mother fussed, cursed, and raised so much hell.

Uncle Louta had no choice but to allow his two sisters to raise Toshiba's son. They would always call him to chastise Tabu, but they wouldn't let their nephew out of their presence nor sight with Louta.

Keisword's mother refused to allow Uncle Louta a chance to corrupt him. She was fearful about him having her three grandsons but by Louta persuading Kawaii and Thy already, there was not much she could do. She was not in the physical nor financial shape to raise all Keisword's sons under the same roof.

Tabu escaped Uncle Louta's criminal influence and that was the only thing that kept peace among Uncle Louta's sisters. They knew they could not save all of the boys but having one that did not follow the family's footsteps was enough to give them all solace.

After having a beautiful visit with his sisters, Uncle Louta's wife Deyarna took him to the doctor's office. There was nothing wrong with Louta, he was in great health and amazing shape for his age. However, his doctor had been recommending prostate cancer screenings since his mid 40's. It was not until his 50th birthday that Uncle Louta began to take his health more seriously.

"How you feel Louta?" asked the doctor.

"Like a King, since beside me, I have my Queen." Uncle Louta replied while looking into his beautiful wife's eyes.

He could see the love oozing out of Deyarna's eyes just as the doctor could see the same effect in Uncle Louta's eyes. Deyarna gave Uncle Louta a smirk and smiled.

"Actually, I'm glad she's here…" said the doctor, "...so she knows what you need to do to take better care of yourself."

"Mmm-hmm." Deyarna mumbled and shook her finger into Uncle Louta's direction.

"Your age?"

"63."

"Height?"

"6-feet"

"Weight?"

"220."

"Louta, how much exercise would you say you get a day?"

"Plenty." Uncle Louta said smiling as he looked into his wife's direction, who was smiling too.

"You are in good shape for your age. Do you feel your age?"

"No."

"Why not?"

"Because I have a beautiful young wife and that gives me

an exemption from them old-man symptoms," Uncle Louta said *being serious, yet sarcastic*

"Now Louta that is a little too much information even for me!" The doctor said laughing, enjoying his patient's sense of humor.

"Doctor, the other old guys need to hear this."

"I'm pretty sure that you'll find some other way than me to get your very important message to them," the doctor replied, returning Louta's light sarcasm to him.

"I don't forget nothing. I'm not senile. I don't need the super-duper strong pill."

"Louta, please…" the doctor continued to smile as Uncle Louta clowned around.

"Louta be good," Deyarna said while giving Uncle Louta the sad face.

Deyarna knew her husband was only playing with the doctor, but she did not feel this was an appropriate time to play. She wanted the doctor to take Louta and his health seriously. Louta read her body language and got serious. Even after all of these years, it was not too much Deyarna could ask from Louta and not receive.

"Yes dear," Uncle Louta replied to his wife and addressed the doctor. "Doc, please forgive me for my nonsense."

"Apology accepted. But I'm not the one you should be apologizing to," the doctor said while slightly nodding over to Deyarna.

"Sweetheart, I sincerely apologize," Uncle Louta said to his wife.

Deyarna nodded and was actually flattered.

"Now with all of that out of the way, Louta let's get back on track," the doctor said as he was taking Uncle Louta's pulse. "Your pulse is good; heart rate beating normal."

"Good," Uncle Louta exhaled.

"Now, Louta, let's get on a more serious note," the doctor announced.

"I'm mentally taking notes doctor," Deyarna said.

"Thank you."

"Doctor, I haven't been sick since God knows when and my blood pressure's been great," Uncle Louta shared. He was there for his six-month checkup, not because of a problem.

"Right, and this is good Louta. You do not have to come to the doctor because something is wrong. One of the best preventive measures are yearly checkups. You are healthy and I want to keep you healthy, so listen. You need to exercise for 30 to 45 minutes a day and at least three times a week. You don't have to over-do it. Louta, at your age, that's all that will be necessary and always obey your body. If you're tired, take a nap; be sure to get your proper eight hours of sleep. Exercise the brain, watch your kidneys, prostate, and cholesterol and most of all, your blood pressure."

"I always check his blood pressure at home, Doc." said Deyarna.

Sometimes, one can say something, and it'll kill a train of thought, but as the saying goes, if it was forgotten it wasn't important.

It was almost as if what the doctor was telling Louta was going in one ear and out the other. He understood the seriousness of the doctor's tone and the concern on Deyarna's face also revealed this was not a playing matter.

"Louta, with your age, you need to always get screened for

prostate cancer because your prostate will swell and get a little bit large at times. Always have a urinalysis and P.A. blood test."

Uncle Louta and Deyarna locked in on each and every word the doctor allowed to roll off his tongue. And they both made one another a silent promise to follow the doctor's advice. Uncle Louta and Deyarna were like two teenagers madly in love. They wanted and needed a couple more decades to be in one another's arms. They took health very seriously and followed the doctor's orders to a tee, however, they paid another doctor a visit to get a second opinion.

***

One hour later, Louta and Deyarna were in the museum, following the tour guide along with the rest of the group. This was Uncle Louta's sixth visit; each time he would appear in disguise, he would never visit dressed as himself. Today, he was an elderly lady, and he wore thick clear lens glasses. He also had a hearing aid in his ear and wore a dress with low cut cloth all white Chuck Taylor's. Uncle Louta was fed up with all the "oohs and aahs" as people would praise the half billion-dollar painting during the tour, but he remained calm and tried to appear just as amazed as the other visitors.

Deyarna was as alert as a newborn baby. Her eyes roamed and soaked her surroundings. She had a small yet very important role to play and it wouldn't take a couple of tours for her to complete her mission.

Uncle Louta walked her through her job. He kept it easy and simple; Deyarna couldn't make a mistake even if she wanted to. Deyarna had butterflies in her stomach; her heart raced over a hundred miles per hour and she had no problems with admitting she was scared and to her surprise, Uncle Louta said he was scared too. Deyarna knew this was a lie, but it did the trick because she stayed a hundred percent focused.

"You don't have to do this if you don't want to," Uncle Louta leaned over and whispered into her ear.

"I want to; I'm with you baby."

"Even dogs have a J-O-B." Uncle Louta said, joking to assist with making his lovely wife comfortable, "Deyarna, Sweetheart, you still look so damn sexy, even -while you_are scared."

"Louta, stop," she said sternly. She could not have her sexy ass husband distracting her from what needed to be done. She could not afford to lose focus.

As the tour guide continued to lead them around the corner of the hallway, Uncle Louta reached out and squeezed Deyarna's booty. One of the males among the group witnessed the play. He told his friends that the old lady and the young lady were bull-dykes.

They had a field day laughing at Uncle Louta and Deyarna until Uncle Louta landed his leather pocketbook across the guy's head, giving him a dose of get right. Uncle Louta cussed himself out for making him and his beautiful wife the center of attention.

"I wonder what babe sees in Grandma?" One of the youngest whispered to his mate.

"Oh no," the girl replied as well as hunched her shoulders.

"Maybe she's hooked granddaddy, because you know granny can remove her false teeth and with them gums suck real good like there's no tomorrow."

"Grandma has been in the world way longer than us," the boy said, as he called himself stealing a glance at Uncle Louta. He looked far too long and found himself getting the pocketbook slammed dunked on his head once again.

"Ouch," he cried out.

"That's for not minding your own business." Uncle Louta stated, with evil eyes. "You lil shit turd! You fuckin pervert!"

"Miss, we are sorry," the girl gave an apology, on her boyfriend's behalf.

The female tour guide had caught wind of the commotion. "Is there a problem? Can I assist you, or anyone with anything?" she asked, but truly she was addressing Uncle Louta.

The tour guide concluded that the young boy was giving the elderly woman problems, probably making fun of her eyeglasses, or hearing aid.

Uncle Louta rolled his eyes at both of the young boys and nodded in an up and down motion to the tour guide while saying, "Yes everything is ok. We good."

"Everything's good, sometimes my auntie likes to get a little too excited, but it's nothing that I can't control," Deyarna confirmed.

"Huh wha'ta you say?" Uncle Louta said, in his elderly woman's voice. "Child is you talking ta me?", he pointed to himself. "You say it's time to eat? Time to take my medication?"

"You have to please excuse my auntie. I hold myself fully responsible for her actions. I can assure you that once I get her to swallow these two lil green pills and drink a cup of prune juice, she'll be back to normal." Deyarna said as she waived the tour guide off.

"Not the prune juice." One of the boys said sarcastically.

Uncle Louta gave him another one across the head. The tour guide immediately turned her focus to Deyarna and angrily said, "You need for me to turn this tour group around and escort you and your auntie to the front entrance?"

"No please don't," Deyarna began, "By all means finish the beautiful tour. I wouldn't allow you to spoil the fun tour for everyone else for the sake of my auntie." Y'all go ahead, we'll find our way back to the front entrance."

The tour guide began to move forward, determined not to delay nor to deprive the others of the full tour. The other guy Uncle Louta hit as well with the pocketbook mumbled loud enough for Deyarna and Uncle Louta to hear.

"You old bat. You old senile bitch."

Uncle Louta smiled, "I hear that," knowing that was one of the comments that he would have to wear. Now with him and Deyarna dismissed away from the group, they could execute plan A, B and C without the slightest interruption. There would be nothing or no one to distract Deyarna once the coast was clear.

Uncle Louta spoke, "God gave you two eyes, two ears and one mouth, so with all that being said do as I do and listen very carefully to my instructions because when the time comes you'll be doing this shit without me."

Deyarna nodded refusing to speak because she wanted to listen to him very carefully.

"Some people can't talk and chew bubble gum at the same time," Uncle Louta said, trying to ease the tension between them by making her laugh.

Deyarna's two eyes watched Uncle Louta, no different than a cat would watch a baby bird that was trying to learn how to fly. He carefully took her through the steps. A couple times back to back until he thought his wife would perform as if it was her second nature and would be successful in this catwalk with her eyes closed. This mission was as if they were only taking candy away from a baby.

***

The museum tours were on Tuesdays and Thursdays. Deyarna and Keisword Jr. entered the building on Thursday. They avoided the tour group, Keisword Jr. wore his military uniform, Deyarna dressed as a pregnant wife, Uncle Louta's voice in their earpiece, "All cameras are now down, it should take no more than three minutes max, to reach the destination. Once you guys are in place let me know."

"Alright Unk."

"Deyarna?"

"Yes, baby."

"Sweetheart, thank you for assisting me."

She forced Uncle Louta to let her go with him on the jobs. To his surprise, Deyarna took to the criminal life as a fish takes to water. She had a few jobs under her belt.

Uncle Louta had already planted his camera's where he needed them on Tuesday. Now the extra eyes would come in handy. He watched Keisword Jr. and Deyarna as they traveled and were their extra set of eyes as he looked ahead of them, so they knew what to expect. "Yes, once y'all bend the corner, we can get down to business," Uncle Louta was talking more to himself, but they could hear him clearly as well.

"Auntie, you ready?" Keisword Jr. asked Deyarna.

"I was born for this shit."

Uncle Louta smiled at his wife's comment, He loved how confident she was, her take charge personality really turned him on.

At approximately 27 seconds later, Keisword Jr. and Deyarna stood before the beautiful paintings. Deyarna immediately unloaded the clothes that made her look pregnant. Keisword Jr. sprang into action racing around to make sure all their play-doh explosives were still in place.

"Unk, everything beautiful."

Uncle Louta replied by starting their countdown.

"9-8-7-6-5" when the number one had been announced the explosives would follow. Next, plan A, B, and C will be executed.

The baby explosives took out the alarm and all the building's electrical power. The water system began to sprinkle everything under the roof

Keisword Jr. snatched the painting off the mount. Deyarna and him raced to another area in the museum and were there in less than two minutes. They just needed to just distance themselves away from the painting location.

Deyarna laid on the floor while Keisword Jr. assisted her with repacking her belly so she could appear pregnant. She began to carry on as if her unborn child was giving her troubles.

"Oh, my stomach. I think something is wrong with my baby," she cried out. Groups of people, and employees raced pass her; they feared for their lives. They did not know what was going on and didn't give a fuck. The explosion had some people's ears ringing and hurting. The cold water released from the sprinklers had them fearful they would drown due to the surge of water spouting down and rising on the floors.

"Someone please help me and my wife!" Keisword Jr. pleaded. The sprinkler's water made him look as though he was shedding tears.

His cries and pleas for help fell upon deaf ears. The people just continued to pass them by with the notion of *every man for himself* or *I gotta save my damn self.*

"Someone please call an ambulance!" Keisword Jr. hollered nearly screaming at the top of his lungs.

"Please?" he and Deyarna faked it so damn good, they deserved an Oscar.

Plan B and C unfolded right on queue. Keiray drove the ambulance to the front entrance and Keiwon did the same in the fire truck. They took different routes in the building but ended up at the same destination. Keiray had led his paramedic crew to Deyarna and his big brother Keisword Jr. by listening to Louta's instructions from his earpiece.

Keiwon had to branch off from his fire fighter crew before he was able to meet up with them, but he arrived in time to witness Deyarna being lifted and placed on the stretcher.

"You alright?" He asked his auntie while squeezing her hand.

Deyarna nodded her head. "Yes, thanks for asking."

"Let's get her out of here," Keiray commanded his paramedics.

"Everything's going to be just fine," Keisword Jr. called

himself coaching Deyarna as she laid on the stretcher.

Keiray was pushing the stretcher in record time, but Keisword Jr. did not miss a beat and jogged every step of the way, making sure he did not leave Deyarna's side while maintaining the act of a concerned husband. Once they reached the front entrance, Uncle Louta was standing there dressed in a paramedic uniform. He'd be in a different ambulance back doors open.

"Sir, I'm glad you're here." Keiray said, in his professional voice. "We can use your expertise to assist this pregnant young lady while we hurry to the hospital." Deyarna nodded, giving Uncle Louta the sign that everything went according to plan.

"You guys can head back, I'll ride back with the patient," Keiray said, dismissing his crew as Deyarna was being loaded into the ambulance. Uncle Louta climbed in the back with her. Keiray raced around to the driver's seat while Keisword Jr. occupied the passenger seat.

Police cars began to storm and patrol the museum perimeter, every law enforcer the small town had flooded the scene.

As soon as the explosives took place, the tour guide fought like hell pushing and shoving herself through the fearful and hysterical crowd. As they fought to exit the area, she was working her way to the billion-dollar painting. Once she reached the empty mount, she screamed into her walkie talkie.

"Stop! Thief!, Stop, Thief. I repeat Stop! Thief!"

"Please repeat?" someone responded.

"The paintings gone mutherfucka!!! Somebody done stole the shit. Ain't this bout a mutherfuckin bitch," she shouted, allowing all of her professional character to go out the window because now she would be out of a sweet babysitting job. Her ghetto side was a hundred percent back, "Fuck, fuck, fuck," she shouted in the walkie talkie.

CHAPTER 5

Pete went to Narma's office to see what he had on his agenda for today, but he only found Narma's face buried into a neat pile of papers that occupied a large portion of the desk. Narma was busy trying to help a dear friend that was behind on taking care of her business.

"Let me find out you went from super-agent to super secretary," Pete joked as he stepped in the office.

"Pete if you were behind on your paperwork hell I'd assist you as well," Narma said looking up briefly from his stack of work.

"I came to kick the boo-boo," Pete said, pulling up a seat in front of the large desk.

"I'm buried knee deep in the boo-boo," Narma joked back with a slight chuckle.

"So, what brings you over?" he asked as he laid the pen down to lean back into his chair and give Pete his undivided attention.

"Just wanted to drop in, check on you, and see what you have on your plate for today?"

"Pete, I told the secretary that I'll devote at least one hour of my time to help her catch up. She is really behind so I may need to squeeze in two hours," Narma replied, he was starting to second guess the promise he made to the secretary.

Pete decided to get straight to the point. He realized his friend did not have much time to spare, "I wanted to hear your take concerning them nuclear warheads?"

Narma let out an exasperated sigh, he moved the paperwork aside and took time to find his words, "If they land in the wrong hands there is no telling what will happen…..some country or enemy will be in a world of trouble. Whoever murdered four scientist and high jacked seven nuclear warheads need to be executed by a firing squad." Narma stood up to stretch, "The fifth scientist will surface soon. If his body doesn't show up - he must have been the inside connect. There is no other explanation of him surviving. We find the fifth scientist; we find a case."

"How is it possible for North Korea to allow the seven missiles to slip through their fingers without a trace? Can the warheads even be tracked?"

"Good question partner, I'm afraid I'm not a scientist. I don't know jack shit concerning the warheads," Narma said sitting back down to focus on his stacks of papers, "We can ask one of our guys in that department. I'm pretty sure that they'll be able to answer your questions."

Narma wasn't trying to be rude, but he had to kick Pete out of his office. If not, he wouldn't be able to fulfill his obligation to the secretary.

As soon as he parted his lips to drop the bomb on Pete, the guy who got his old detective job knocked on the office door. Narma walked over and opened the door.

"Detective Top, how nice of you to drop in on me," Narma said as he shook the young agent's hand.

"You remember my old partner, Pete?" he asked, gesturing

towards Pete.

"Yes sir. How could I not remember one of our hometown heroes?" Detective Top turned to shake Pete's hand. "Agent Pete, how do you do sir?"

"Fine son and thank you for asking," Pete said as he returned the firm handshake.

"So, Detective, what brings you into my neck of the woods?" Narma asked. He did not want to be rude, but he was just about to get Pete out of his office, now he had two unwanted guests and a secretary's job to do. What a damn day he thought to himself.

"I was in the neighborhood and decided it wouldn't be law if I didn't pay you a visit." Detective Top lied.

Narma read Detective Top's body language and knew he had the young agent's full attention- the young guy was ready to listen to anything Narma said.. So, he fired off another question which should've been his key question, "So Detective please tell me honestly how's the job coming along?"

Detective Top produced a fake smile.

"Bingo," Narma exhaled, "What's the problem son, you drove way over here to ask me what? Or to unload your burdens? Come on, spill your guts.

The Detective did not have to be told twice. He enlightened Narma and Pete about the museum robbery and was wondering if Narma had thirty minutes or so to review the surveillance video collected from the museum as evidence. Top and his crew watched the video for hours and were completely lost. No leads, no ideas, no motives other than money, no witnesses, no nothing. He had to go to the best for help, only to solve the case.

"Sir, your expertise is greatly needed," Detective Top explained, "I was advised to seek your counsel sir, because you were the best of the best."

Narma loved the young Detective's words, in reality, he loved that he was so good at his job it was hard to find a replacement for him, but he didn't have time to hold the novice's hand and he didn't have time to entertain Pete. Today was his lucky day. He could kill two birds with one stone. He could get Pete out of his hair by asking him to assist Detective Top.

"Agent Pete here has been my partner for decades Son. He will be able to assist you with the same expertise no different than I could," Narma said smiling.

Pete hopped to his feet, "Young man it will be an honor to assist you and besides our partner Narma is the secretary-in-charge for today." Pete told Detective Top as he looked over his head and began to tease Narma, "See ya and right now I don't want to be ya. If you not too busy would you be kind enough to bring us a pot of coffee and a box of donuts, we have a case to solve…. you are just filing paperwork right?"

"Pal right plan, but wrong man," Narma said, with laughter and quickly shuffled both men out of his office.

Once Pete and Detective Top were seated in the conference room, Detective Top brought the TV screen to life, showing all the visitors as well as the tour groups.

Pete nearly choked on his own saliva. He instantly recognized Deyarna and Louta's name written all over this billion-dollar painting heist. But the young agent did not have the eyes nor nose to see and smell these career criminals.

"You can cut the TV off now," Pete requested.

"Did you see something sir?"

"No, did you?"

"No, sir, that is what brought me here today. I have been reviewing the tape for hours and can't even get a good starting point," the young detective admitted sounding defeated.

"Son, do you at least have the list of all the people that visited the museum?" Pete wanted to help, but damn, he didn't realize this was going to be a tutoring session.

"Yes, sir," Detective Top answered quickly as he removed the papers from his briefcase and replaced the video back into the briefcase. He could sense the irritation in Pete's voice and the last thing he wanted to do was rub his help the wrong way.

"Son, did you look over all the lists?"

"I wanted to wait until I was here with agent Narma."

Jesus, how did this kid move up to detective? Pete mentally questioned himself, as he scanned the list. He saw what he did not want to see- on line 47 of the visitors sign in list was the name Deyarna Williams.

Louta Williams getting sloppy or he's getting too damn old for these criminal activities. He thought as he continued to drag his trigger finger further down the list with his eyes following. Pete went over the ten sheets twice to see did his own two eyes fail him by only producing Deyarna's name only once. Since Pete couldn't get Narma to play secretary for him, he turned to the young Agent and knew Detective Top wouldn't decline.

"Son, would you please be kind enough to go back to Narma's office and get us a fresh pot of coffee and one of them stale boxes of glazed donuts?"

"Sure, no problem sir. I'll be back in a flash."

As soon as the detective left the room, Pete hopped on the desktop computer and retyped page six. Now he began to count his blessings for taking the typing class because it finally served its purpose. Because he was able to type over sixty words a minute. By the time Detective Top emerged back through the door he was long finished and could've retyped the whole ten pages.

"Nothing like coffee and donuts," Pete said, as he poured himself a cup and dipped the donut into the coffee twice, before eating a big bite.

"Mmm," Pete mumbled, "son you don't like coffee and donuts no more?"

"Thanks, but no thanks. I ate pancakes for breakfast with my daughter," Detective Top lied, only his daughter ate pancakes. He was too busy trying to get in the presence of Narma. So, he skipped breakfast all together.

Pete began his interview, "So Detective how much was the painting worth?"

"I was told a billion."

"You see anybody on the video? Anyone you think would be a suspect?"

"No."

"You looked over and listened to the video to see who all visited the museum more than once in the same month?"

"I looked over it briefly."

"But neither studying nor analyzing, am I correct?"

"Yes," Detective Top was realizing his rookie mistakes and was becoming embarrassed. But he continued to answer all of the questions Pete asked. He knew he only had himself to blame for not being prepared.

"If you had to put a suspect in mind who would you point the finger towards?"

"The female tour guide."

"Detective Top, would you please look over this list for me," Pete passed page six over to him, "Would you be kind enough to read the forty-seventh name to me?"

"Dewanda Walter," Detective Top said, as he stared hard at the name. Wishing he could erase the name with his eyes.

"Does her name ring a bell?"

"Yes sir."

"Why Detective?"

"Because she was my first love! My high school Sweetheart," Detective Top managed to blurt out. Just the thought of Dewanda brought tears to Top's eyes and rage to his heart. He was trying to keep his composure, but it was hard to do.

She was also on the same page he was on in the yearbook and Pete was secretly hoping Top would lose his cool at the mention of her name. Detective Top provided a little too much information, so Pete used the entail to re-open some old wounds.

"Detective Top, I'm afraid that we're out of time please feel free to drop in anytime you need to," Pete exited the room without trying to shake the young Detective's hand. He wanted to dismiss himself so the guy could have his privacy to lick them old wounds.

***

Three hours later the F.B.I. director held a conference with his agents that were assigned to the terrorism operation. He wanted them to receive first-hand knowledge of the top ten America's most wanted and most powerful people. The man with the snow-white beard and hair was the most powerful and destructive amongst them all. He was known to kill his co-defendants with kindness and his blinding smile. The Tycoon wouldn't let you hear it, he'll let you see it, he'll let you feel it, and will demonstrate his alphabet, where the letter I came before U.

The director showed five photos of the Tycoon, all the pictures of him were on one of his twin boats.

"Director, Sir, why are all his pictures on the yachts?"

"Because he thinks he's the Pirate of the Sea," replied the Director.

A different agent raised his hands.

"Speak," the Director gave permission.

The guy stood and began stating facts none of that he says she says shit. "The man is a tycoon. He has twin yachts that cost him anywhere from five to eight million apiece. He made his fortune by any means necessary. He doesn't take no jobs less than a million or better. He's tied to crooks all over the world. He doesn't give a damn about what you need done or want. If the price is right, he's your contact man. He contracts people to do all the dirty work. He's too wise to get his hands dirty. The Tycoon allows his money to work for him, he refused to work for the money. He's famous for buying stolen goods then he auctions them off to the highest bidder. He'll transport cocaine, heroin, guns, and human beings. We estimate the man is a multi-billionaire. Only God knows what he wouldn't do for the dollar." The guy sat back down giving the Director back the floor.

Reese whispered to Narma, "The Tycoon, the Tycoon, the Tycoon,"

Pete mumbled to himself as he stared at the man's photo with evil eyes. He began to study the picture. He wanted the Tycoon's image ingrained in his memory.

"He's powerful," Narma reminded.

Another agent raised his hand.

"Please stand and share with the others," The Director encouraged.

The guy stood and gave his portion.

"This slime bag has been caught by us several times. Also, by the C.I.A. as well as the Coast Guards. All he can't pay off he'll work off. Meaning he'll give them someone to take his place. His favorite phrase is *It's better him than me.* The guy is a snake!"

"He's a snake," Pete said, "Well, we the mongoose and mongoose eat snakes."

The agents began to cheer and whistle.

"Agent, you must be one of the new guys?" The Director said, "Because around here we don't do the outburst thing. Agent if you have something that needs to be said please raise your hand. And I'll give you the opportunity to voice anything you feel we need to know."

Pete raised his hand.

"Stand and speak agent," The director instructed.

Pete stood, "Sir, I apologize for my outburst." He did not want the director to think it could've been Reese or Narma. Pete was twenty-one concerning the situation.

"Thank you, agent, for coming clean," the Director said, "Please finish."

"Sir, how is it possible we constantly risk our lives and co-workers' lives to catch these hard-core criminals and y'all let them snitch their way back out of the situation if not pay their way out?"

"Agent, sometimes this thing can become bigger than me. Prime example," the Director began to explain, "The Tycoon is not just a crook. He's extremely intelligent. It never fails, every time he's arrested; he'll have some important info that the bureau or C.I.A needs. He knows how to bargain for his freedom. He is always a step or two ahead of us. He can weasel his way almost out of anything. That is what makes the situation so frustrating!"

"Negotiate my ass," Pete mumbled, as he reseated himself.

The agent sitting two seats down from Narma raised his hand. Since Pete was on a good topic, he wanted to elaborate.

"Speak," the Director said.

"Sir, when is all this 'snitching their way-out' mess going to come to an end?" The agent asked not realizing snitching and negotiation comes along with the territory.

"Good question," Pete mumbled.

"Great question," Narma whispered.

"Let's see what the Director has to say," Reese said in a low tone so only Pete and Narma were able to hear him. Even though Reese spoke in hushed tones, the agent next to Reese still strained to eavesdrop on their mumbles, whispers, and comments.

"Agent, as I have said previously, sometimes these things can get bigger than me. You guys answer to me and I have other heads over me that I must answer to. Now with that being said, I'm pretty sure I wouldn't have to address this issue again."

"I can assure you Sir; it won't come from me again," the agent replied while dropping deeper into his seat.

"Thank you, Agent. It does my heart good to hear that," the Director said, but truly he was addressing them as a whole and not that agent individually.

"Find the Tycoon. Plain and simple. He is the source. If we find the Tycoon, it will slow down a lot of crime. He entices these young fearless criminals to steal goods. He will purchase the stolen goods and re-sell them for half of the price. When you find him, ask him about the jacked nuclear warheads. If he didn't have someone do it; he knows something about it. I'm so sure of it that if he doesn't, I'll place my own head on a chopping block."

"He always admitted to the role he played in the crimes." The agent seated next to Pete shared with him spilling the beans immediately. "When we get into his presence. He always has some strong evidence on ice for us."

"It never fails huh?" Pete said.

"Nope."

"You heard what the Director said, he'll put his head on the chopping block," Narma reminded them.

"The director oughta know," Reese said.

***

11 P.M.

Three dozen agents huddled around so they could see the location Pete was touching on the mounted border map. He brushed his fingertips lightly across the map tracing one angle to another as he spit out instructions. Since he made that outburst, the bureau director made him the commander over Unit A.

"Narma, you, Reese and Unit B head towards the north and if our technology is on the money, one of the Tycoon's ships will be sitting in the water like a baby bird sitting in its Momma's nest. Me and my team will head towards the east coast where the other yacht should be sitting like a duck."

"What all are we supposed to find?" Narma asked.

"Guaranteed drugs, a few million in cash and about half of a hundred beautiful women." One of the agents said. He knew what to expect because he was a part of the raid twice.

"Oh my God," another agent slapped his forehead and said, "Geisha," in a voice with pleasure.

"Geisha." Pete repeated.

"What is Geisha?" Reese asked.

"That name means female Japanese entertainers," replied another agent who was amongst the raid as well.

"Interview all of the girls," Pete instructed, "because we need all the info we can get and use against the Tycoon."

As the other agents began to pair off, Reese and Narma walked over to Pete.

"Agent Pete, I have a joke about the Tycoon, you care to hear it?" An agent in his unit asked.

Pete wasn't in the joking mood. Truly, he could care less about the joke and wanted to tell the agent where he could shove the joke. But Narma spoke for Pete, "Sure let's hear it?"

"You know why the Tycoon's hair is snow white?"

"Why?" Reese asked beating Narma to the draw.

"Because he's always worried about us," The agent said,

laughing at his own joke.

"I doubt that very seriously," Pete grumbled.

***

1:37 A.M.

Narma, Reese and fifteen more F.B.I. agents with two boat loads of Navy Seals boarded one of the Tycoon's Twin Yachts.

As predicted, there were a few dozen beautiful female models from all around the globe. Tons and tons of heroin, cocaine, weed, and guns. Five million in small, well-sealed plastic bags containing hundred-dollar bills but the Tycoon was nowhere in sight.

It would be a very long morning because everyone on the ship had to be interrogated. The interrogation was more of a routine. Everyone knew it would be a waste of time and money. The Tycoon had ingrained the fear of God into their memory banks - they weren't going to tell anything. The law enforcers had nothing to lose and everything to gain. They would bless the people to spill their guts in order to try to help themselves.

"You think Pete knew this ship wasn't the one the Tycoon would be on?" Narma asked Reese and wanted his honest opinion.

"Why would you think like that?"

"An old agent instinct," Narma replied.

Reese was inspecting the drugs. He knew Narma was waiting on a response, but he was waiting to be face to face with the Tycoon. He didn't know what Narma was trying to imply, but right now that wasn't important. They missed their chance to nail one of the most infamous criminals in history. This would have been the biggest bust in their careers. "But you are not a detective anymore. We are all F.B.I. Agents. Reese replied sternly. He didn't want to choose sides and he did not have time to play the guessing game with Narma.

"You still haven't answered my question," Narma said.

Reese could see the challenge in Narma, "You think Pete wanted to take the credit for putting the Tycoon behind bars?"

"Let's just say I have a hunch that it's more than what meets the eye," Narma said. As he pressed the button on his walkie talkie to report to Pete.

***

2:37 A.M.

Pete, twenty-five F.B.I. agents, and a boat load of Navy Seals looked through their night vision goggles as the boats sped towards the Tycoon's ship.

The Tycoon could smell the law closing in on him and some of his men threw a large portion of drugs overboard. They punched holes in the barrels so they would sink to the bottom of the ocean.

All the law enforcement team boarded the ship safely without any trouble. Everyone immediately got within compliance. They knew they were in a world of trouble and if they played their cards right, while they were knee deep in shit, they could come out smelling like a rose.

"Locate him, and immediately report to me." Pete instructed his team.

"We know he's yours Sir," A Navy Seal guy replied, "He'll

be in your custody."

"Everyone spread out," Pete ordered, "My personal unit stay with me."

The guys paired off in small teams of four, they rushed to go and find the big bad wolf as he played hide-n-seek with them.

Pete heard Narma trying to contact him on his walkie talkie. He turned the walkie talkie off and commanded the other F.B.I. Agents with him to follow suit. Monkey see monkey do.

Normally it would've taken a couple hours to search the entire ship. The Tycoon could've hidden from them, but he knew eventually they would find him. But this time he surrendered without putting up any resistance. He walked slowly towards four heavily armed Navy Seals, with both arms held high.

"Hello boys. I'm unarmed and I come in peace. I love Jesus, how about you guys? I'm pretty sure we can settle this misunderstanding." The Tycoon was the only one smiling, the four officers' faces were made of stone, his words fell on deaf ears; but that didn't stop him from continuing to press his luck.

"How much would it take to make this misunderstanding go away? A million? I know, how bout I make each of you guys a millionaire? I'll give each one of you a million dollars right now?" They still didn't respond. "Who I gotta pay? Who I need to pay?" The Tycoon continued. "Do you toy soldiers know who I am? You do know I am an important man with great powers."

One of the Navy Seals responded by hitting the Tycoon in the mouth with the butt of his machine gun. Knocking him unconscious. His spilled blood hit -the floor before his body.

They dragged the Tycoon's body to Pete. Another of the Navy Seals threw a bucket of ocean water in the Tycoon's face bringing him back to life.

"How nice of you to join us," Pete greeted.

"Who is you?" The Tycoon asked, as he tried to wipe the water from his blurry vision and the blood from his sore mouth. He had never encountered Pete before; he began to think to himself that they were trying to play the tricks on him again. Which he always learned and forgot once he paid off their fee. He was accustomed to other law enforcers who ruffled his feathers a little.

"I'm your worst nightmare," Pete replied, pulling out half of a chewed cigar before striking the wooden match on the match box. He looked at the Navy Seal and motioned for him and the others to leave, "Me and my guys need to be alone with this piece of trash."

"Here we go again with this top-secret shit," exhaled the Navy Seal that knocked the Tycoon unconscious.

"Yeah." Pete agreed. He was applying fire to the cigar and puffing like hell as if it were giving him trouble to light. "Top secret shit," Pete said while blowing out the cigar smoke.

"Top secret my ass," another Navy Seal said with an attitude. He told his crew over and over they should've taken the Tycoon's offer because they wouldn't be the first nor the last to do it.

"Pal, I'm afraid you're in a world of trouble," Pete said.

"How could you say such a thing? When you never been among a man such as my status?" The Tycoon asked. Truly he wanted to try to give some orders but something about Pete's presence told him, he better start talking and talking fast.

"Mr. F.B.I. man please tell me, how I may accommodate you?" The Tycoon smiled out as he snapped his fingers. "The nuclear warheads will make you a hero if you are able to locate them."

"A hero huh?" Pete asked with a laugh.

"It'll make you a big man amongst your peers," The Tycoon stated.

"What else you have to offer?" Pete asked, playing along with the Tycoon's game.

"Money," the Tycoon said, "and I do mean a lot of it."

"I'm going to ask you a question. If you're truthful it can be the beginning of a beautiful relationship or it will be the end of what could've been a beautiful relationship," Pete said as he looked at the Tycoon with hateful eyes.

"What you want to know?"

"How much cash you have on this ship?"

"A little over thirty million," the Tycoon immediately announced. To him, this amount was bird feed or simple pocket change he kept on board to pay off law enforcers and make his troubles wash away.

Pete put the barrel of his weapon into the Tycoon's mouth and pulled the trigger, scattering the elder guy's brain without one bit of emotion. Afterwards he contacted Narma to report the Tycoon's death.

"Narma. I had no choice but to kill him."

"What do you mean?" Narma asked, as he walked away from the other officers. He motions to Reese to follow him, so he'll be able to listen to him and Pete.

"He had too much money and power. Narma this was the only way we would've been able to stop him. Now we wouldn't have to worry about his wealthy rat ass again."

"Pete?"

"Yes," Pete said, but he didn't like how Narma just said his name.

"I'm with you when you're right," Narma began, "I'm with you when you're wrong. I just hope that in the name of God that you're not too wrong." Narma stated as if he just unloaded his troublesome burdens.

Narma and Reese talked amongst themselves.

"Narma, I pray to God that Pete's ego doesn't turn him into a killing machine." Reese said and hoping like hell that he did not talk things into existence because as for the record four out of ten of Pete's suspects were killed upon their arrests.

"The killings always take place when we're not with him," Narma reminded. "Now you see why I said what I said."

Narma readjusted his vest, "Pete will always be one of us."

"Narma. I'm not saying he switched sides," Reese stated.

"You're trying to say he's playin both sides? Good cop and bad cop?"

"Maybe or maybe not," Reese stated, "Let's continue to watch him and not rule out the possibility."

CHAPTER 6

D.B. Jr. wasn't the best dresser, but he dressed average. His mother wasn't into the fashion thing, he never wore a pair of Jordan tennis shoes because to Crystal that would be a week's worth of clothing. D.B. Jr. was a small 14-year-old boy who minded his own business and stayed in his own lane. He did not have many friends; you could count three at the most. He wasn't a problem child. He was raised to be respectful and polite.

How he managed to get on the bully's radar, his schoolteacher and a couple of his friends would like to know.

D.B. Jr. rode his bike to school against his grandfather's wishes. As he was securing his bike into the bike rack, the 15-year-old bully took off, giving him a swift and solid punch to the head. D.B. Jr. was no match for the muscular teen but that didn't stop him from trying to fight back. The bad guy swept, mopped, and painted the floor with D.B. Jr.'s young ass. Every time D.B. Jr got knocked to the ground, he would get right back up and continue to fight.

After the fight, the other students gave D.B. Jr. pats on the back and words of encouragement.

"Good fight man. You showed the bully you wasn't backing down."

"You gonna be alright lil bro?"

"Man, you got heart."

"Boy, if you would have been a little bit bigger, you would have taken him."

"Lil one, you ain't got to worry about him trying you no mo."

D.B. Jr. wore the ass-whipping like a champ, he did not speak ill against the guy nor did he speak any foul language. He politely hopped back on his bike and peddled back home. Once he arrived home he counted his blessing that he walked into an empty house, everyone had already left for work. He went straight to the location where he watched his grandfather hide his pistol. D.B. Jr. then rode his bike back to school, walked into the building and entered the bully's classroom and emptied the whole clip into the bully's upper body. He did not give a damn that it was broad daylight, or that there was a class full of witnesses, he just wanted to get his man. He hogged up a mouthful of mucus and saliva, he spit onto the bully's dead body.

As D.B. Jr. was getting booked and charged for the murder, the teachers, principal, and students talked among themselves because no one saw this coming.

"That child wouldn't kill a mosquito," stated a teacher.

"Not even a roach," another teacher said, as she recalled a flying cockroach flew into the classroom and landed in reaching distance for D.B. Jr., she instructed him to kill the four-legged creature and D.B. Jr. declined stating it ain't bothering him.

"Never in a million years, I would've thought that child would carry out such a murder," said the principal as he spoke with disappointment.

"That child had a very good heart. He was raised by a good family," insisted the teacher who knew D.B. Jr.'s grandfather and his mother, Crystal.

"He's not a cold-blooded murderer. He's not this monster that this crime portrays him to be. We've got to take into account the bully beat him senseless and Williams shed not one tear. He forced the youngster to act out with rage."

The teachers were in the faculty's lounge trying to make sense of D.B. Jr.'s murder when the students were in the cafeteria speaking in hushed whispers.

"Son, lil one is a cold gangsta. He did not say one word, he just walked into the classroom and opened fire. He taught Mr. Bad Ass a helluva lesson bout fuckin with him."

"I can't believe he did it," A female said, as she cried into both palms.

"Fuck that punk he needed killing," A male student said out of anger because he had been the bully's victim for the last two years. He wished death upon the bully more than anyone else. But he didn't have the guts, nor heart to be the trigger man. He silently saluted D.B. Jr. and quiet as kept D.B. Jr. was his hero. Before the week was out, he told himself, he would drop D.B. Jr. a few lines confessing his support along with a few dollars for whatever he needed on the inside.

"We all have to testify on Williams behalf," stated another female. "Because he's not the devil if anything the devil made him do it." She spoke out of love, lust, and concern. And to her surprise everyone amongst the small group agreed.

When the officers were questioning the students, everyone spoke highly of D.B. Jr. and in his favor. The entire school thought he caught that body by force and not by choice. He wasn't a troublemaker, never encountered a run in with the teachers, students, nor the law. He was a quick learner and stayed on the A-B Honor Roll.

Once the school notified Crystal on her job. Afterwards, she cried like a baby knowing damn well her tears wouldn't be able to assist her only child. She did not know if she was going or coming. Crystal's mind went completely blank. Now her worst nightmare and biggest fear were able to come to reality.

Crystal was in a catch 22, stuck between a rock and a hard place. She had done the best for her child. Now she was forced to go against her own will and against the law of nature. Crystal bit into her bottom lip as she dialed the seven-digit number, by the time the phone began to ring, she could taste her own blood.

"Hello, this is the Williams residence, how may I assist you?" Keisword Jr. said.

"May I please speak with Louta Williams please?"

"Unk phone," Crystal heard Keisword Jr, say and moments later, she heard the strong deep and creepy voice.

"Hello, Louta speaking."

Crystal remained silent and let a few more tears escape her eyes.

"Hello, hello, Louta Williams speaking?"

"Your grandson has just been hauled downtown to the county jail and he's been booked for murder. I was told that the bully beat him nearly half to death and D.B. Jr. went and got a damn gun from somewhere and went back to school and killed the boy. Uncle Louta please save my child! He is s all I have left of D.B., please Louta, I'm begging you?"

Before Uncle Louta could respond or ask any questions the line went dead,. only because Crystal had spoken her peace and hung up the phone in his face. She couldn't bear to go thru a question and answer session with Uncle Louta. Not right now maybe some other time, right now it would be like pure torcher to her.

Uncle Louta wasted not one second of his time. He immediately phoned his lawyer giving him the little information he just learned along with D.B. Jr.'s full name. The lawyer was upset by Uncle Louta's instructions and tone of voice.

"Get my nephew a bond. I don't give a flying fuck whose ass you have to kiss, or whichever one of them dick heads dick you have to ride. But make it happen today and not tomorrow!"

The lawyer did not like the way Uncle Louta was talking but there wasn't a damn thing he could do. He was wise enough to know he put himself in this situation when he sold his soul to the devil.

"Louta this thing is not as simple as you think. We are talking about a murder case here and we'll have to start off playing the situation by ear and…"

Uncle Louta interrupted the lawyer's sentence; he wasn't trying to hear anything he had to say. Uncle Louta needed him to listen, when he was ready for counseling or advice, he'd ask for the input.

"I need you to get him a bond," Uncle Louta gritted and closed his teeth. "I need him in my custody today. So, let's fucking worry about today and that way you can leave all the worry up to me for tomorrow!"

The lawyer swallowed his pride. He did not wear his emotions on his sleeve. He reminded himself this disrespectful shit and fucked up attitude come with the territory of angry clients.

"I may know a friend of a friend who may be able to get us a bond. The Judge will probably set the bond anywhere from five hundred thousand to a million dollars."

"I don't give a damn if it's a million or two million get me the fucking bond. We'll pay cash," Uncle Louta said.as he fed the lawyer the dial tone because there was nothing else needed to be said.

The lawyer sat there in his chair thinking, *Louta always wanted things done that are always difficult to do.* But from one angle or another he always managed to get the job done. Louta always has him exercising power or influence that he did not know existed; as long as there's a will there's a way. The old gangsta forced the lawyer to live up to his full potential. The lawyer would cuss and fuss within himself but deep down inside of him, he praised Uncle Louta for giving him the extra push that was needed.

"It's nothing a hoe wouldn't do for a dollar," the lawyer said out loud, because he needed his ears to hear his own joke.

Before he began calling around asking for favors, as well as cashing in favors. He made Louta top priority, the head of his agenda. Louta would and could be bitchy at times, but he always pays and tips like no other. Triple O.G. was in a class of his own.

Seven hours later.

The lawyer phoned Louta stating the million cash bond has been set. Louta thanked him as well as promised him that his cooperation would not go unrewarded. Louta immediately phoned the funeral home, because soon and real soon there was going to be a lot of flower bringing.

***

Detective Cain and Detective Abel were supposed to interview D.B. Jr. concerning his situation, but they'd so much animosity against Uncle Louta that basically their whole conversation was about him.

Since Uncle Louta was always getting away scot free, they were wishing, hoping, and praying that this young member could be loose at the lips and assist them with sinking Louta's ship.

"Son you know your Uncle Louta Williams is a person of interest in over seventy-one murders," Detective Cain stated, as he stared D.B. Jr. in the eyes while twirling his thumbs.

"Louta has been a criminal his whole life," Detective Abel said, as he studied D.B. Jr.'s face.

He needed D.B. Jr. to give them a piece of information they could add to their arsenal or to unconsciously give them some kind of lead. So, they could bring the Williams criminal empire to an end.

"Louta has corrupted your whole family and if he's not careful, he'll corrupt the Williams up and coming younger generation," Detective Cain said, as he looked at Detective Abel.

"Louta has to be stopped."

Little did the Detectives know that D.B. Jr. had never ever met this so-called Monster Uncle of his. Uncle Louta never existed until now. His mother nor grandfather didn't mention one word of his father's side of the family. Now he began to see why. The more and more the Detectives bad mouthed Uncle Louta, the more he began to admire this gangsta Uncle of his. Once he caught a glimpse of some females on the news and if he could recall, it was some guys also and their last names were Williams. His grandfather changed the station so he wouldn't hear what the news was saying that day.

"Louta gave you the pistol and told you it was ok to kill the bully," Detective Abel said. Trying to put words in D.B. Jr.'s mouth.

"Now that sounds like something Louta would do," Detective Cain added, backing up his partner's words.

"Louta keeps plenty of firepower handy."

"Louta, ain't give me shit," D.B. Jr. shouted, as the veins stood erect on both sides of his neck, "I ain't no snitch."

Detective Cain hopped to his feet, "Tonight when we put your young ass in one of them cells. -Your lil young ass going to be one of them convicts sweet little sexy bitch."

"I'm nobody's bitch," D.B. Jr. railed, "I'll kill again."

The Detectives watched in disbelief as the youngster stood before them foaming out the mouth. His anger and disdain for the detective was so malicious they would not have believed he never met Louta or any of the Williams for that matter.

"You're a wild ass animal, no different than Louta," Detective Abel said.

D.B.Jr. did not take the words as an insult. Instead, he accepted it as a compliment because it connected him amongst his true family.

"The Williams are not above the law, I'll hunt them all down one day and I refuse to rest until I carry out justice to its full capacity, by crucifying you all," Agent Cain said with animosity. The hate could be smelled from his breath and seen from his glassy pupils.

"We'll crush all you fucking Williams, like the fucking cockroaches that y'all are." Agent Abel said. He wouldn't sleep good tonight if he wouldn't spoke what's truly on his heart.

D.B. Jr. sat back down into his chair because common sense told him, he couldn't out talk these cops. So, he did the next best thing that was within his power, he began to think how beautiful it would be to come face to face with Uncle Louta, because as of now he wanted to praise the man's name. And counted his blessings that he had the same last name.

The small office phone rang. Detective Cain answered and ended the brief conversation.

He exhaled, "Baby alpha male, you're saved by the bell," he faked a smile, "Your fancy lawyer is here to get you."

"He got bail so soon," Detective Abel said, with an attitude, knowing this would come into play.

"Yup." Detective Cain said, while sounding off the letter P sound.

"That's Louta Williams's work," Detective Abel said as he playfully snuffed into the air.

"I can smell Louta all over it," Detective Cain laughed, "Louta knew this lil' punk would've broke down and cried."

"I'd rather shed blood before I shed a tear," D.B. Jr. stated and meant each and every word.

"You are -saved by the bell lil' boy," Detective Cain said as D.B. Jr's lawyer walked into the room.

"Now, you guys know better than to question one of my clients without me being present," the lawyer said as he placed his briefcase on the table.

Detective Cain held up his right palm, "Mr. Expensive Babysitter, you got it all wrong. We just were utilizing these few minutes of fame as entertainment."

"Yeah…just entertainment," Detective Able agreed, producing his best fake smile.

The lawyer disregarded the two clown agents because he was aware of their character.

"You didn't allow them to trick you into making a statement?" He asked D.B. Jr.

"NO way Jose," D.B. Jr. said. He nodded towards both Detective, "They two sissys."

"I heard that," Agent Cain said. D.B. Jr. gave them the finger.

"If your lawyer would've been a day later. You would've hung yourself in that cell. I can see you now committing suicide." Detective Abel said smiling.

"Us Williams don't do suicide, we do homicides," D.B. Jr. stated and was serious as a heart attack.

***

Uncle Louta sat on his front porch. He saw his lawyer driving down the dirt road toward his home.. He'd seen D.B. Jr. many times from a distance. Now, -he looked forward to meeting him and to get better acquainted. They didn't want to give him D.B. Jr. upon birth. But, due to this tragedy, he'll be able to raise D.B. Jr. along with Keisword's sons.

As the lawyer began to park ten feet from the porch, Uncle Louta got up from his chair and began making his way down the steps.

D.B. Jr.'s heart was about to jump out of his chest. It beat so hard and so fast that it gave him a headache. He exited the vehicle nervously. D.B. Jr. sized Uncle Louta from head to toe and thought, *"He look so dangerous to me."*

Uncle Louta saw all of D.B.'s features, the child was a spitting image of his father.

"Louta is there anything else that you need me to take care of?" the lawyer asked from behind the steering wheel.

Louta approached the vehicle, reached in his pocket, and retrieved two crispy fresh bundles of hundred-dollar bills from his front pocket and dropped them onto the lawyer's front seat. "That's twenty thousand extra for your troubles. Now scat, I know where to find you when I need you."

The lawyer smiled, "Yes Sir, I'm always at your service Mr. Louta Williams. I'm only a phone call away," the lawyer said before driving off.

Uncle Louta threw one of his arms around D.B. Jr.'s shoulders, "What you think about your lawyer?"

"Is he gonna get me off the hook?" D.B. Jr. asked nervously as they watched the lawyer travel back down the dirt road.

"You mean beat the case?"

"Yes, Sir."

Uncle Louta laughed, hoping it would be the medication to ease the tension that burdened his nephew.

"Son don't allow that to trouble you. That's not your

problem anymore." Uncle Louta patted himself on the chest. "That's my problem now and what we both can call water under the bridge."

"Why you say that?"

Uncle Louta laughed again because of the nervous child's voice, "Because you are a full-blooded Williams."

"What about my clothes?"

"Your mother will bring all of your belongings over tonight." Uncle Louta said and guided the conversation to the subject the agents were throwing at him left and right.

"Son, you didn't make no statement, did you? You know not to say anything that will incriminate you?"

"I told them why I did what I did."

"Why did you do it?"

"He uh…. he kept bullying me."

Uncle Louta patted him on the back, "Nephew, you did the right thing. I would've done the same thing."

The butterflies in D.B. Jr.'s stomach vanished, Uncle Louta's strong words of encouragement were enough to strengthen his soul and convert his sad face into a smile.

"Unk, them agents called you Diablo. Unk, what does Diablo mean?"

"It's Spanish for the Devil."

"Unk they talked real bad about you," D.B. Jr. reported. But in his mind and heart, he found the detectives words to be impressive. The words also made him very proud and honored to be Uncle Louta's great-nephew.

"Son that won't be the last time, you hear them shit down on my name. They always talk bad bout us Williams."

"Unk?"

"Yes."

"You think them police gonna come here and get me and take me back to that jail?"

"Not unless it's over my dead body. Son, I'll keep you beside me as if you' are my shadow."

"You got my back Unk?"

"Yes son, I got your back."

"Then I got your back too."

Uncle Louta escorted his nephew through the house. D.B. Jr. noticed the gold and silver metals and studied them longer than necessary.

"What you got them for Unk, swimming?"

"I was a sniper, while I was in the service."

"So, you can shoot real good huh?"

"I hit bulls-eye every time. Son, I don't miss."

"How can I get like that?"

"Son you'll be five times better by the time I'm finished with you."

"You promise?"

"Son, I have to even against my own will because one of these days, my life may depend on it."

CHAPTER 7

Deyarna lay silently on Uncle Louta's chest and listened to his heartbeat while he poured out his heart and vented about his great-nephews. Keisword's three sons: Keisword Jr. was the oldest, then Keiwon and Keiray was the baby. Deyarna· was sorry and excited concerning D.B.'s son's tragedy because now the family was complete.

"Sweetheart?" Uncle Louta called out to his beautiful young wife while hugging her closer to him and kissing her forehead.

"Huh?"

"You sleep?"

"No."

"Why, you so quiet?"

"Cause, I'm listening to you," Deyarna stated the honest to God truth.

She felt guilty for not bearing his children. Even though Uncle Louta always put her nerves to rest by saying he was too old and not physically able to teach and play sports with his babies. On the few days he did play with Keisword's sons, his body paid dearly the next day, his back and knees would be the main source of his troubles.

Uncle Louta filled in all the blanks for Deyarna concerning D.B. Jr. and his case. She had faith her husband would play puppet master and pull the right strings as always. It never failed. So, when he told D.B. Jr. don't worry about the situation, Louta actually meant the problem was a thing of the past.

"Deyarna, I love them boys."

"Me too," Deyarna confirmed as she lifted her head up to plant a wet kiss on Louta's lips while gently stroking his penis.

Louta wasted no time pulling her on top of his growing manhood. Deyarna straddled his hard dick and slipped him gently into her wetness. She moaned softly as her throbbing clit pulsated on Louta's manhood with each up and down motion. Without losing her rhythm, she placed both feet flat on the bed and began bouncing on his dick. She wanted to drive Louta crazy and she needed her g-spot stroked. Her plan worked. Louta moaned in ecstasy while her love juices rained down his dick and created a small puddle under his thighs.

Her body quivered from the orgasm she just experienced. But Louta wasn't done. He quickly flipped her over and began fucking her doggy style. Deyarna couldn't take the long thick strokes, she knew she was about to cum again.

"Louta, I am about to cu-cu-cummm," she managed to say between her moans of pleasure and pain. "Cum in my mouth," Uncle Louta commanded while pulling his dick out and diving face first into her love pot from the back. Once Deyarna felt Louta's swift tongue sucking, biting, and licking her wet pussy. She lost control. Her body exploded like a volcano and she laid paralyzed in her own moisture. She did not even know if Louta came, but she was too weak to even ask.

"Sweetheart, I needed that."

"Ummh," Deyarna moaned "and me too."

"Seconds would be nice."

"You gonna need ya energy. Tomorrow them boys gonna have ya butt wide open," Deyarna said and raised her head up to give Uncle Louta a passionate kiss sucking her juices off his sexy lips.

When it came to her pussy, Uncle Louta was more of a giver than a receiver. He got his satisfaction by pleasing her. Him and Deyarna stayed in the 68, she'll be forever in his debt by owing him one.

They quickly fell asleep. Both exhausted from their love making.

Around 2AM, Uncle Louta was awakened by the heavy rain and baby lightning. He carefully eased out of the bed and got dressed.

He then went into his nephew's rooms to wake them up., "Y'all dress in all black and meet me in the kitchen in ten minutes."

His nephews weren't even sleep for a full hour. They were up half the night trying to make D.B. Jr. feel at home and get to know him. They described Uncle Louta as the perfect father figure. Keisword Jr. explained that the old man was hard on them because he loved them and everything he did was completely out of love. He explained that Uncle Louta always pushed and encouraged them to be the best they could be and most of all he wanted them to be a better man than their father and him. D.B. Jr. asked plenty of questions because truly he felt like Uncle Louta had his best interest at heart from their previous conversation.

The four boys stood in front of Uncle Louta wiping sleep from their eyes and taking turns yawning. Uncle Louta saw them as Gangsta Slim, Risgo, PK, and Keisword. They remained silent and patient for the wise old man to speak his mind. D.B. Jr. was scared and nervous. He put his hands behind his back and toyed with his fingers.

"Sons, it's time we go out in the rain and practice," Uncle Louta looked into D.B. Jr.'s eyes as he talked, "Since the detective said I am an animal, from this day forward, we will train like one. That way we'll always be more advanced, more powerful, and stronger. This will separate the people from us Williams. We'll always be able to survive because we will train hard and smart."

With that being said, he led them into a wooded area on his property. Uncle Louta had them performing as if they were a fresh batch of Army recruits. He ran and trained them on an empty stomach. D.B. Jr. started complaining and Keisword Jr. quickly let it be known that the old man, like hearing all of that bitching and hated hearing D.B. Jr. ask, "when will this show be over?"

Keiwon told him, "Whether you like it or not, we will not throw in the towel until Uncle Louta says so."

Uncle Louta gave them weapons with rubber bullets and commanded they hunt down one another. This game consisted of shooting one another. The winner will be the man who shoots the most people.

"I don't know how to shoot from a distance," D.B. Jr. confessed.

"Then you better learn cause you gonna be their target

practice," Uncle Louta warned, "and son, by the time I get finished with ya, you'll be able to shoot a fuckin falling star out of the sky."

D.B. Jr.'s little legs were already hurting due to this being his first rodeo. But little did he know this was going down in history as the Williams Tradition.

The weather forecast said it will rain for seven days and seven nights straight. The rubber bullets promised to leave red marks all over D.B. Jr.'s body. Uncle Louta invested quality time into D.B. Jr., so he was able to qualify as a good shooter among Keisword Jr. and his brothers.

Uncle Louta was surprised that D.B. Jr. continued practicing even after he had told them that they had had enough practice for the day. He scored excellent on hitting the target from a distance, he immediately advanced by hitting the bullseye of the targets when they were hunting deer, squirrel, rabbit, and other moving targets. D.B. Jr. took pride in his shooting. He wanted to be the best.

He took to shooting like a fish took to water. By the end of the week, he had red marks on the backs of all three of Keisword's sons.

Each one of Uncle Louta's nephews specialized in something that the others couldn't touch with a six-foot pole. D.B. Jr. knocked Keisword Jr. out of the box, Keisword Jr. did not player hate, he only congratulated and cheered his cousin on by saying, "That's what us Williams do." Uncle Louta did not show any favorites. He treated them all equally. Keisword's sons treated D.B. Jr. as if he was their biological brother. Uncle Louta told himself that D.B. Jr. was the missing link to completing his family.

***

A month and six days later Doc stretched and warmed his leg muscles before taking off to complete his five-mile run as he would do every other day. He began this ritual when he became borderline diabetic. He started taking the proper steps because he did not want to graduate to the insulin shots and certainly not to the dialysis machine. His doctor explained through diet, eating properly, exercise and losing weight, he can get off the 500 milligram pills as well by burning off more calories than he takes in.

"Hello Doc," the young lady greeted as she began to follow his lead, especially since he led by example.

"How are you today young lady?" Doc returned the greeting as he watched her perform the same stretch he previously did.

"Doc, you was the doctor that delivered me when I was born," she said prideful since her mother pointed it out this morning.

He delivered many babies, as well as was custom to hearing this sentence. So, he stuck to the script.

"That's the only talent God gave me. So, if I may ask what you do for a living?" This is how he managed to get all of the focus off of him.

"I'm a dentist and I'm also into real estate."

"I-I-I, oh my God, you are multi-talented," Doc said, smiling.

"God gives some people one talent. Some two talents, and some even get three talents. I model as well. I'm trying to become the next super model in my division."

Doc looked at his watch and began jogging in place, "Young lady, you are a multitasker. You are aware that running can keep them pounds off you. Also jumping rope is good because you'll be exercising every muscle in your body. It burns off a couple hundred good calories. I always do this to warm up my old bones."

She followed the Doc's stride thinking since he was a doctor he knew what he was doing, but for the sake of his health he'd need to be educated on how to watch his sugar intake as well as how to burn off the sugar.

Doc told the young lady that he bet a salad with chicken breast chunks he would outrun her around the trail and back.

"It is a bet," she replied.

Doc waived his right hand through the air as he bowed. "Ladies first, so please take off because I'm going to spot you two car lengths." Doc knew he couldn't beat her in the first place. The slick devil was only trying to get better acquainted.

"See ya and don't want to be ya," she said and set out to be the winner because being a loser sucked. The young lady breathed through her nose which was the proper way to breath while running. She ducked several times to avoid limbs as she raced through the woods.

Doc jumped over a rotted tree as he tried his best to stay on her tail, but to no avail, the lead he gave her grew by ten car lengths because she was a natural runner.

The Doc put more pep in his step trying to close in the distance as Uncle Louta and D.B. Jr. lay on the roof of a corner building. Louta's blood was boiling with anticipation as he watched the Doc through his binoculars "Come to Poppa," Uncle Louta exhaled. "Doc, I warned you that once a Williams get a taste of blood, they become a vampire and crave more blood. We always get our prey. You brought my son into the world and now my son will take you out of this world."

Sweat was pouring down D.B. Jr.'s face as he looked through the rifle scope. The Doc was a hundred and thirty-two feet away. The sweat was causing D.B. Jr.'s eyes to get blurry for a brief second, but he was afraid of losing his target, so he refused to blink with each of Doc's jumps or ducks, D.B. Jr. was glued and zoomed in on him.

"Son, no bird, no squirrel, no rabbit, no deer has escaped you. Now it's time you give the doctor a taste of your wrath. Since he failed to obey my instructions"

"On ya call Unk," D.B. Jr. said as he finally began to breathe again after a few seconds. He was holding his breath because he thought breathing would take him a slight bit off his target.

"He'll be coming around the mountain, when he comes," Uncle Louta sang, trying to take some of the tension off his baby nephew. "Let the son of bitch have it son. This unworthy piece of shit is only soaking up good air."

D.B. Jr. tapped the hair trigger three times, hitting Doc in, the center of his forehead, and into the both eyes. The first bullet did the job. D.B. Jr. wanted to show off his skills. "Oh," Uncle Louta allowed to escape his lips as he watched the doctor's legs give out as if he'd tripped or stumbled over a tree. "Oh, oh, oh," Uncle Louta breathed again upon watching the blood spray from doc's face. His soul and spirit felt relieved upon seeing the Doc's dead body hit the ground.

"Our business is done Unk?" D.B. Jr. asked because he wanted to knock the girl off for being in the wrong place at the wrong time.

"I'm afraid so son," Uncle Louta replied. "Our damage is done; we got our prey. Now our man no longer is a thorn stuck in my ass."

"Unk, did I earn a gold medal today?"

"You certainly did."

"Now I gotta work my way up to a silver one."

"Is that a problem son?"

"No sir," D.B. Jr. said without hesitation. "I wanna be the best shooter."

"Son, that's exactly what the service did to me and to be honest with you being the number one snipper is all I ever wanted.

CHAPTER 8

Agent Reese was twenty states over, but he still subscribed to his hometown newspaper, especially since he discovered one of the Williams was facing a murder charge. He wanted to see how Uncle Louta was going to 'Houdini' his great-nephew out of the court's hands. If there's a will, he will find a way, and this, Reese wanted to see.

Reese read the papers from cover to cover, but the obituary always came first, then the rest will follow. Today was his off day and the top of Reese's agenda was to read all of the two weeks' worth of old papers. He allowed them to stack up due to their high-profile cases. After reading six of the papers, his consistency finally paid off. D.B. Jr. died in a house fire and he'll be buried on Friday. Agent Reese was stunned. A creepy chill traveled through his body.

"Friday, Friday, Friday," He mumbled, truly talking to himself because he lived alone. "What day is it?" he continued talking to himself. "Thursday!" Reese answered. He studied the time and place of the burial and immediately notified Agent Narma.

"Hello, this is Agent Narma speaking, how may I assist

you?" Narma answered his desk phone.

He was in his office. He was only working a half day. His body wouldn't allow him to rest if he didn't look into the jewelry store robbery one last time. While at home Agent Narma's mind always revisited his cases crime scenes which helped him break the cases.

"Narma, this is Reese"

"You ain't been off two hours yeyet and you miss me already?" Narma joked.

This new case was like a thorn in his ass. He wanted to cry instead of laugh.

"Remember the Williams boy's case?"

"Reese, you'll have to accept my apology for not following you," Narma said as he closed the file he was going thru. He leaned back into his chair and propped his feet on the desk so he could give Reese his undivided attention. "I'm all ears pal."

"Louta Williams great-nephew- killed the bully?"

"Yes, yes, now I'm with you," Narma replied "So what did the magician do now?"

They always used the word 'Magician' or 'Houdini' when referring to Uncle Louta.

"For some strange reason, his nephew came up dead."

"He did what he do. Reese I am sorry I don't follow you." Narma said.

"He killed his nephew."

Agent Narma's brain went into overdrive. He's been dealing with crooks since high school. He learned in order to catch them; he had to think like them. He remained silent because he was thinking. The information Reese just dropped on him did not add up. It made no sense at all.

"Narma?"

"Yes."

"You heard what I just said?"

"Yes, Reese but that doesn't sound logical, it doesn't make any sense."

"You're right," Reese said.

"You thinking what I'm thinking?" Narma asked.

"The slick devil's faking his nephew's death," Reese said, revealing his theory.

"Bingo," Narma said. "What else do you have?"

"The funeral is tomorrow at one o'clock," Reese said, while looking around his one-bedroom duplex.

"We have to book us a flight and be on the next thing smoking back to South Carolina," Agent Narma said. "I'll book the flights and call you back after I talk to Pete."

***

The day of the funeral Agent Narma sat behind the wheel. Agent Reese occupied the passenger seat. Agent Pete played in the backseat of their unmarked black sedan parked two hundred feet from the grave site. Agent Narma unlocked the latches of his briefcase and pulled out a black object that was the size of a Pepsi can but was heavy as four rolls of quarters.

Narma switched the button to ON and placed the device on his dashboard. The TV's in the sun visor and on the back of the front seat headrest immediately came to life. As they stared at the screens, they became in the midst of the burial. They could see everyone's face and hear every word that came out of every mouth.

"We'll study everyone's face," Agent Narma began, "to see if the Career Criminals and the Ridaz show up to pay their respects, since they most definitely are the Risk Takers."

"The Williams Boys and the Williams Girls," Agent Reese said.

"They're not just a family, they're a functioning family," Agent Pete remarked.

"They all will get the lethal injection together," Agent Narma gritted out of clenched teeth.

"More likely hold court in the streets," Agent Pete said as he began to study Uncle Louta's eyes from his live TV stream.

"Yeah, Narma. I agree with Pete. I don't think they're going to allow us to bring them in alive." Agent Reese added his input.

Agent Narma knew his agents were speaking the absolute truth because he told himself the same thing. They just were able to beat him to the punch line by allowing it to roll off their tongues first. Agent Narma feared for that day to come because just as sure as there's a God in heaven, it will be a very bloody day because blood will be shed, and a super-large funeral will follow. Besides, this is what law enforcers signed up for.

Some days he actually wanted to throw in the towel and call it quits. Retire and enjoy the rest of his life in peace with his wife and loved ones. But his heart and conscious wouldn't allow him to take the easy way out. Agent Narma invested so many years chasing and thinking like Uncle Louta and the Career Criminals that now he felt as if the only thing that could stop him is his casket being lowered six feet under.

"Narma, you think they'll have the nerves to show their faces here?"

"Reese, they have nuts, even the women."

"They'll do shit that people in their right frame of mind wouldn't even think of doing," Agent Pete said ready to fill his lungs with smoke. His body was craving nicotine.

The agents studied every face and listened to every conversation that went on. They kept the device aimed in Uncle Louta's direction at all times, hoping he would make the smallest of mistakes.

Agent Narma recorded the entire funeral and every word that came out of Uncle Louta's mouth. Uncle Louta did supply some small whispers here and there but that was all so far. Agent Narma did not give up. He knew he wouldn't leave here empty handed. He knew that Uncle Louta would slip and provide that smallest bit of evidence that is needed to nail himself to the cross.

"Honest to God, I think the man practices covering his fucking trail in his sleep," Agent Pete said.

"Every time we think we have him, he slips clean through our fingertips." Agent Reese said.

Agent Narma did not like how they were giving Uncle Louta credit where credit wasn't due.

"So, in other words, what y'all two tryna say, they running a circle around our asses?" Agent Narma asked.

"Yes, Sir. A complete circle," Agent Reese replied, because it spoke for itself. It was fact.

They did not have a single one of the Williams's in custody and only four of them in the graveyard.

"Guys, it's been a long day and I think the flight has taken a toll on our brains," Agent Narma said, as he was becoming angry behind another one of these wild goose chases.

"I say we get some machine guns and gun Louta's ass down. Then justice will be done. Then when the other Williams come out of their fucking rabbit holes, we fucking gun them down in the same manner." Agent Pete said. He was serious. He didn't give a damn how his partner took it. "Shit, we'll win and be scott free of harm's way."

"We'll be inheriting their insane ways," Agent Reese said.

"We just need to try to bring them to justice and waste as little blood as necessary." Agent Narma said, calling himself looking out for their best interest.

"JUSTICE," Agent Pete shouted, "justice my ass. The word justice is like the word joke when it comes to the Williams Family. You know it, Reese know it, and I know it."

Agent Reese whipped his hand over his eyes and face, "Guys, it's been a long day and we wasted two hours here. We need to get us a good night's rest and tomorrow we'll be able to put our heads together and finish what we started by taking down these clowns by any means necessary."

"I agree," Narma agreed.

"Narma, I apologize for going overboard," Agent Pete said, "sometimes we have to learn to put our feet into the other guy's shoes."

"I did that the day one of the Career Criminals walked into our county jail and broke the girl out in broad daylight and murdered the extremely trained captain on the sidewalk." Agent Narma pointed out, as he mentioned the work of Gangsta Slim.

"Very unfucking predictable," Agent Reese said.

"Williams don't fear death, they only welcome it, or more so, embrace it," Agent Pete said.

"The guy went into the county jail," Agent Reese whistled, "it takes steel balls."

"That kind of shit don't suppose to happen in a million years," Agent Pete said in a complaining tone.

Agent Reese looked into Narma's eyes, "Guys, we are not enemies here. We are on the same team and have the same agenda. Which is to take down all animals and to cease their unnecessary bullshit."

"Shit don't stop till the casket drops," Agent Pete said, eager to get in the last word.

Reese sometimes can be dealt with, but Narma, he's one hundred percent by the book. He's dedicated to his word and upholding the law. Narma is also the highest-ranking agent among them. Reese agreed with Pete. But Pete will never know because Reese's loyalty always remains with Agent Narma and that goes without question.

***

Keisword Jr. told his brothers Uncle Louta is a genius. He said them pigs would come snooping down their funeral-line. Everything Uncle warned them about has come into existence. Now they see the old man don't just talk because he had a mouth. Uncle Louta actually took them step by step and coached them on how to act and speak during the funeral.

"The person sitting next to you could be an F.B.I. or C.I.A. agent. They're going to study your every move as well as start a frivolous conversation. Remember, loose lips sink ships. They're going to always have eyes on us from a distance. Keep your antennas up sons and eyes open. When one of you see a strange vehicle parked a distance from here it's gonna be them. Ask me for a handkerchief and fake like your blowing your nose so we all can be on point. My senses may be off, but you all are young, so I may need each of you to be my eyes and ears."

CHAPTER 9

The girls lounged around in Toshiba and Nifitinma's room. They all lived in expensive suites. Toshiba did not like to be cooped up; she's wild and full of energy. Lagonda passed the bottle of champagne to Faydra so she could fill her glass. Since she skipped her turn of playing waiter as rest of them had done.

Toshiba hit her blunt a couple times before passing it to Nifitinma. Nifitinma liked to be around Toshiba because Toshiba knew D.B. better than anyone. She was always telling her stories about him. Toshiba told the girls many things about her and D.B., but she wasn't crazy nor high enough to tell about the time her and D.B. were pumping gas.

D.B. was outside of the car and two girls pulled up. The passenger started talking shit to D.B., saying how she would suck and fuck his brains out. D.B. never afraid of a challenge told her to run it up then and stop fronting.

Toshiba had asked D.B. what the fuck she was supposed to do while he go and unload his nut? D.B. told her, "Bitch, let the other bitch give you some head. If a bitch will suck a pole, she'll damn sho eat out a hole." Toshiba took one for their two-man team.

Even though, now days it's cool and accepted to be a lesbian, Toshiba still wasn't coming out of the closet. She was taking that one to the grave with her. Truly she is not into pussy, that was her first and only experience. She went along because of D.B.. But on the flip side, her baby daddy asked her to do a threesome or let him watch a female eat her pussy. Toshiba called him everything but a child of God.

"Sitting up in a hotel or motel month after month, this shit gets old," Toshiba said as she put ice into her glass and refilled it.

"I agree," Nifitinma said.

"My baby said we was going to the Dominican Republic and he was going to rent us a mansion for about a month," Lagonda let the cat out the bag, as well as altered Gangsta Slim's sentence because he clearly said that he was thinking about it.

"Either there or Jamaica," Faydra released what Risgo told her.

"Mmmuumh," Toshiba moaned while taking a couple large swallows from her glass, "'I need to get me some of that Jamaican dick or Dominican dick. Child, they got them accents that turns me the fuck on. I will even give an ugly one some of this pussy." She began dancing nasty, "I'll have that Spanish muthafucka talking in Spanish while he sucking my pussy. "

"Girl, you are wild," Nifitinma said.

"I just do what grown folks do," Toshiba replied.

"Dominican Republic is better than Jamaica," Lagonda said to Faydra.

"More room, more privacy," Faydra agreed.

"Tell y'all men when y'all doing that lil pillow talk

something need to be a group discussion." Nifitinma said and nodded towards Faydra and Lagonda.

"You right," Lagonda said.

"Bitch, you got a fuckin mouth, tell'em ya damn self," Faydra said, smiling.

"Bitch, you know I will," Nifitinma said as she rolled her neck.

"I'm glad you said that. Now that will be my topic of the day when I talk to Risgo and Gangsta Slim. hit, I needed something to talk about anyway." Toshiba said and began to sing out, "Jamaica or Dominican Republic, here the fuck I come."

***

When Lagonda got back to the room Gangsta Slim was laying on the sofa and talking to Mr. Kibble on the phone. They would talk for hours daily and sometimes Slim would drive them two states over and take Mr. Kibble sight-seeing. He couldn't keep Kibble with them because Kibble would be dead weight on one of the others if they had to bail out or shoot their way out of a situation.

Gangsta Slim was the only one who would be able to keep the bomb building scientist cool, calm, and collected; otherwise, Kibble would panic to death. Somethings were old to one and brand new to others.

When Gangsta Slim and Kibble were in hibernation two months straight. They would the watch uncut videos that came on at 2 A.M. Kibble fell in love with Video Soul, Rap City, Sanford and Son, The Andy Griffin Show, and the Price is

Right. All of this was intriguing to the scientist because Yan Kibble spent sixteen to twenty hours daily working on a bomb. He had no life and lived on bases and compounds. All he ever knew was work and go back to his one-man living quarters which consisted of a bed, table, and a shower. There was no TV, or phone. There was an intercom in his room, but Yan Kibble never talked to anyone other than the security.

Every blue moon he'd be burdened with the responsibility to explain why their product wouldn't meet the deadline due to the other scientist not being knowledgeable enough to deliver the speech out of fear.

Mr. Kibble taught Gangsta Slim a great deal about technology. He showed Gangsta Slim things that wouldn't be exposed to the world until five to twenty years from now. Mr. Kibble was ignorant to life in general, but with space, equipment, building bombs, and working on rockets he, was a pure genius.

Thanks to Uncle Louta, they were tied to criminals all around the world. Uncle Louta had a mean and very powerful connection. This is how Gangsta Slim was able to put Mr. Kibble up. Yan Kibble's picture stayed on every news channel around the world. The C.I.A. and F.B.I. were on his trail and like always the trail got cold because Uncle Louta's crew of Career Criminals and Risk Takers' business partners were the definition of death before dishonor. If they gave up a member, their family can kiss the world goodbye.

Mr. Kibble knew he was on the run and was wanted. But the crazy man would always tell people his real name. In his field, he was so smart but yet so stupid. The word bored didn't apply to him because since day one he was isolated from society. His living always consisted of no more than a prisoner in solitary confinement.

One man's junk is often another man's treasure. The people around Mr. Kibble would give him broken TV's, radios, and other appliances. With the broken equipment, he would build microwaves, dryers, washing machines. Mr. Kibble refused to allow any machine to be smarter than him. He was going to make it work and do what he wanted it to do. He was the people's handyman.

Mr. Kibble was so accustomed to wearing his long white sleeve shirt and black slacks, that Gangsta Slim had to lay his clothes out daily on the bed for him. He had to reprogram Mr. Kibble. He actually babysat the scientist, so Kibble learned to depend on Gangsta Slim and Gangsta Slim alone. Mr. Kibble wasn't hip to using the telephone. The device (as he called it) was the only way he was able to close in the distance and put himself in the presence of Gangsta Slim. The only man he loved, respected, and treasured as a dear friend. Gangsta Slim showed Mr. Kibble loyalty from day one and in return- he received Mr. Kibble's loyalty.

***

Lagonda walked over and laid on top of Gangsta Slim. She whispered into his free ear, "Tell your scientist friend goodnight because I need some love and affection," she did not have to tell him twice. He immediately gave Mr. Kibble their goodnight farewell. He was ready to say hello to his lovely wife's kitten.

She did not waste any time. As soon as he hung up the

phone, she shoved her tongue all down his throat. Gangsta Slim could smell the weed on her breath as he sucked the alcohol off her tongue. This turned her on so much she couldn't wait to put all that pussy on him. But she was in for a rude awakening.

Gangsta Slim didn't need any pills or alcohol to boost his sex drive. A nepho did not have shit on him. and to Gangsta Slim, it was his law of nature not to allow a woman to outdo him. His psychopath demeanor would automatically kick into overdrive and against his will, he was going to punish her body; put a hurt on her vagina for trying him.

Lagonda nutted so much that she lost count. Gangsta Slim beat her twat sore and until she repeatedly begged that she couldn't take any more. But her plea fell on deaf ears. Gangsta Slim had done zoned out, while pushing in and out of her body.

When he came back to his senses, he sincerely apologized. "Baby, I'm sorry. Sweetheart, I love you and I promise it'll never happen again."

"You got my pussy and stomach hurting."

Instead of telling her he was sorry again, he decided to show her. He began to softly kiss her thick thighs while caressing her plump breast. He used his tongue to make circles that lead to her sweet smelling pussy. He knew she was still sensitive and so he kissed her pussy softly.. His mouth healed all of Lagonda's pains. She completely forgot all about being hurt. All she saw were stars and birds flying in circles around her head. She arched her back and locked her legs around Gangsta Slim's neck, while moaning, "I Love you, I Love you, eat my pussy, ohhh, I'm cummming. Please don't stop, ohhh, this ya pussy, this feels so damn good." Gangsta Slim tongue fucked her to death, keeping the love of his life chasing her breath as her chest rose and fell.

Lagonda was lost and confused. She did not know which one was the best his dick, or his tongue. After about forty-five minutes of constantly cumming and talking in tongues she began to whine and also beg for the dick again. Lagonda loved wet pleasure in her ocean that only Gangsta Slim could deliver.

"Slim?"

"Huh?"

"Please fuck meeee," she pleaded, while trying to pull his head away from her pussy and she needed him to shove that phat and long tongue of his down her throat. So, she could taste her own milk and honey which always turned her sex game up a notch. Lagonda purred the word, "Mmmm," into Gangsta Slim's mouth as his manhood filled her to capacity, fitting into her pussy like a glove. Lagonda's breath escaped her body with each and every pound, "Uhh, uhhh, uhhh." The wetness of her vagina had a tone of its own.

"That's right ba-by," Lagonda began losing control, "get this pus-ssssy, make mmme cummm on your diccckkkk."

A devilish smile spread across Gangsta Slim's lips because he told himself, it's time to give Uncle Louta another son. He palmed both of Lagonda's butt cheeks. Gangsta Slim long stroked her and focused more and more on her g-spot.

With each stroke her pussy got louder and louder. Her noises were about to make him cum. He quickly pulled out his throbbing dick and smacked across her smiling pussy, giving special attention to her fat ass clit. Lagonda lost her mind while he continued to rub the tip of his dick over her clitoris before diving back deep into her wetness. Lagonda held him tightly and bumped him like crazy because she was cumming all over again. Honestly, she couldn't get enough of him. She was addicted.

"Gangsta, you make me cum so much," she confessed, while lightly scratching his back.

"Sweetheart, your pussy is so damn good, I don't want to cum. I want to stay buried inside you," Gangsta Slim said, as his dickhead began to spray freely, fertilizing the eggs needed in order to bring forth life.

CHAPTER 10

Seven days later they finally arrived in Montego Bay, Jamaica. Gangsta Slim took Mr. Kibble along with him. His first priority was to take out the G.P.S. out on all their phones as well as anything else that could track their location. Besides, Mr. Kibble wanted phones to do whatever he wanted them to do if he wasn't in full control - he was going to find a way to be.

Mr. Kibble refused to allow anything technical to be smarter than him. His favorite saying was, If God wanted machines to be smarter than man, he would've given it the brain." Mr. Kibble hacked into stranger's phones for entertainment. He loved anything that gave him a challenge.

Risgo had to meet the people Uncle Louta had set up to give him all the weapons needed. Weapons and protection were Risgo's expertise. Risgo could break down any form of weapon and rebuild it in record time. By training the group of Career Criminals it gave Uncle Louta more love and respect in their worldly crime ring.

Nifitinma, Toshiba, and Faydra toured the beautiful resort, this was a true vacation for them. Water from a mountain flowed around them into a stream that formed into a swimming pool at the resort.   AS the young ladies were enjoying their leisure time, one of the young Jamaican hustlers approached them. "Ganga? Ganga?" He asked them twice while placing his fingers to his mouth as if he was smoking. They did not know what in the world he was talking about, but his motions were understood very clearly.

"Ganga," the Jamaican hustler said once again. This time he took off his backpack and pulled out a clear plastic bag full of weed. long. There were sticky bugs all the way around it, from top to bottom.

"Ten American dollars," he said.

Toshiba gave him a twenty-dollar bill and told him to keep the change. All three of them together still couldn't smoke over a thumb's length of the leaf rolled with bugs. They were good and high. The pub was a small bar and wasn't hype enough for them. Toshiba' s wild ass talked them into going to a club, she sipped on a blue muthafucka. Nifitinma had an incredible hulk and Faydra enjoyed her Jamaican rum. They sat back taking notes as the Jamaicans danced their asses off. The women did a sensual dance called the *dirty wine*. They moved their hips in a circular motion- fast and slow, slow and fast- however the beat made them move. The men were right behind them dancing, not missing a beat. Some couples looked like they were fucking on the dance floor.

Toshiba got so turned on watching the sexual dancing her pussy began to drip sweet juices messing her thong panties up. She couldn't contain herself for another second, for another minute. She hit the dance floor and tried her best to durty wine - between the blue muthafuckas and the weed, she was courageous and didn't give a damn about who was watching her. A Jamaican man with dreads to his waist began to dance with Toshiba. a. She was no match for him, but that did not stop her from trying to fuck him with her hips. They grinded and hunched on one another. He licked behind her ear and she was melting in his arms. He added fuel to the fire gently placing the tip of his tongue in her ear while slowly taking in her addictive scent.

"Some people can dance their ass off, but can't fuck worth shit," Toshiba said with her no dancing ass.

"Are you a freak?" He asked, with a small hint of Jamaican accent that was difficult to detect. He spoke so clearly and concisely; it was easy to tell he was educated

"It depends on how good you can eat and beat the pussy, and besides, I'm a Williams. We are animals." Toshiba said proudly. She looked like a no dancing drunk white woman on the dance floor, but she didn't care and continued to dance her heart out.

Faydra and Nifitinma had a field day laughing and crying watching Toshiba's drunk and high ass. The other Jamaican guys on the sideline watched Toshiba with lustful eyes. Thinking about how they'll spend long hours on that American pussy. Even some of the Jamaican females thought about a one-night stand with Toshiba..

"I'm a rude boi and to you that would mean, I am Mr. Lover man," he whispered in her ear. He introduced himself as Ivory and he wrapped his hands around Toshiba's waist to pull her closer to him. He slow wine and grind on her so intense, she thought they were having sex on the dance floor. Toshiba's panties were soaking wet and her body was at his mercy. She would've paid him well for some dick. Ivory was wise enough to know the effect he was having on her. Toshiba wasn't the first and surely wouldn't be the last who got hypnotized by his seductive ways.

"Fuck all of this teasing," Toshiba said, "I want to see how you perform ass hole naked," she was getting ready to beg for the dick because all of her hormones were acting up.

"Like a champ," Ivory replied, smiling, "I talk it and walk it."

"Bullshit ain't nothing, let me see it and not hear it," Toshiba said, grabbing him by the hand and leading him off the dance floor.

"Your room or mines?"

"Yours would be better," Toshiba replied, because she wanted to keep her lustful ways out of Gangsta Slim and Risgo's sight.

"Before you leave my bedroom, I want to pierce your clit," He said.

"Anything for you, darling," Toshiba quickly agreed, she didn't want anything delaying her unexpected dick appointment.

***

Toshiba laid with her head hanging off the bed. Ivory was trying to shove all ten inches of his dick down her throat. She gagged a few times, but once she got her mouth wet enough and the rhythm of his stroke, she was taking all of his dick with ease.   She loved sucking dick and would cum just from pleasuring her partner. She was more of a giver than a receiver and Ivory loved every minute of it.

Toshiba had taken control of his manhood as she worked that neck. He came quicker than normal. All she did not swallow, he sprayed over her face which also was a turn on for them both. Toshiba gave his dick a couple more sucks before he told her to turn around so he could taste the pussy.

"I love how your big ass dick stretched the back of my throat," she moaned. "You got a pretty dick."
She hoped he knew how to use that tongue of his to show her some appreciation. She spread her legs on the king-sized bed. Ivory licked across her clitoris, teasing her. His tongue made her back arch and that was the position Ivory told her to remain in. He French kissed her throbbing pussy with his wet lips, tickling her clitoris with sloppy kisses and sliding his tongue in and out of her dripping pussy. Toshiba was losing her mind cumming back to back. She want him to fuck her - it was as if he read her mind. He slapped her pussy with his hard dick. Her juices instantly covered his manhood and he effortlessly slipped inside of her. "Fuck me," she begged.

Ivory began feeding her hungry pussy his dick, inch by inch. He felt like he was in pure heaven and quickened his pace. "Oh god, this pussy good," He moaned. Toshiba arched her back and threw that pussy back. After a few deep penetrations she began nutting like crazy. She bit down on her bottom lip and her eyes rolled behind her eyelids as orgasms washed and flooded through her, "Get this pussy!" she purred.

"Girl this pussy tight," Ivory said, "and good as a muthafucka."

They weren't in a nut race. her hidden agenda was to out fuck one another - make the other one tap out. There was no love making involved, just straight fucking. Ivory knew it was best to put Toshiba on his fifteen-minute rotation because if he didn't, he would cum faster than normal. He'd fucked plenty American women but Toshiba, was too much for him.

Ivory pulled out of her and instructed Toshiba to lay on her side. He slightly pushed her top leg over bending her knee a little allowing easier access to her pussy. This time he was far too gone to switch positions. The nut was on the top of his dick. The pressure and feeling was too damn good to delay any further. He pulled out and began jacking off as cum shot all over Toshiba's ass and thighs. When Ivory finished milking his dick, Toshiba sat up, "let me help you get that dick back good and hard again." She placed his soft dick in her mouth and gently slurped and licked around it until it stood at attention. She then lowered her wet mouth slowly down his hard shaft while humming and using her free hand to massage his balls. He was ready for round two again in no time.

After a good five minutes of fame, Ivory was back in business once again and she damn sure needed him to finish what he started. Ivory commanded her to get in her favorite position- face down and ass up. Now, she would be able to throw her ass and pussy in all directions with nothing in her way. Ivory sank back into her tight walls and began to thrust and pound deeply into her guts. Their powerful blows were equal. Ivory touched and connected with each and every piece of her pussy. The wetness of her pussy was music to his ears and his moaning was music to her ears.

Ivory pulled out and rubbed the head of his dick back over Toshiba's asshole. Once she felt his manhood pulsating back there in uncharted land, Toshiba quickly lost the arch in her back. She turned around and told Ivory, "Ain't nothing going in my ass but toilet tissue. You'll give a bitch fucking hemorrhoids with all of that dick. I'll give you all the head and pussy you want but my ass is off limits. You can tongue fuck it if you want to."

Ivory dove in with his tongue, hoping by the time he was finished Toshiba would have a change of heart. While he ate the booty from the back, he was also successful with the mission of jacking off.

When he woke up in the morning Toshiba was sucking his dick. He could not have opened his eyes to a better pleasure, *Baby wasn't lying when she said she was an animal,* He thought as he laid back and let her do her thing. Toshiba stroked her fat pussy as her eager mouth sucked away. The more she moaned, the faster and harder she rubbed her pussy. As he came in her mouth - she came in her hand. Fuck, this nigga is going to make me stay in Jamaica she thought as she looked at him and slipped her pussy soaked fingers in his open mouth. He stared at her stunned as she finished licking her fingers while telling him, "can't let this good pussy juice go to waste."

***

Agent Pete paced back and forth because he had to make important phone calls that he did not want to make. He was sick and tired of his j-o-b, but he had signed up for this shit and everything else that would come with the territory.

He had put an invisible leash around his neck and put the leash handle into the devil's hands. In so many words Pete had sold his soul to the devil. Now he began to act like one and think like one. Agent Pete's mind stayed fully loaded as the devil attacked and everyone knew the devil refused to let one loose. Agent Pete was faced with one hell of a dilemma and to make matters even worse, the old him constantly battled with the new him. He picked up the receiver and slammed it back in place six times. As much as Agent Pete smoked to calm his nerves and to help him think better, today nicotine was not enough to solve his problem.

"What the fuck should I do? What the fuck can I do?" He actually began talking to himself as he pouted around in his office. "Shit Pete, think! Think got-damn it!"

Agent Narma strolled by heading back to his office with a fresh cup of coffee. "There goes Narma's ass, I been waiting for him to come the fuck back. I wonder where the fuck he been?" Agent Pete continued to talk to himself.

Finally, he picked back up his desk phone and dialed the seven digits. As the phone was ringing, he thought, "don't answer the muthafucka after five rings he told himself that he'll give it one more ring and the phone was answered. Agent Pete did not give the other line the opportunity to say a word. He wolfed out, "WE NEED TO TALK NOW," and used his thumb to push down the plastic button to disconnect their lines. He peeked through his blinds as he watched Agent Narma slam his receiver back into the phone rack as he had previously done. Narma stormed out of his office heading in the direction of his office.

CHAPTER 11

Gangsta Slim, Risgo, and Faydra met privately on the top floor of their penthouse suite. Risgo filled them in concerning the group Uncle Louta had lined up to assist them. Risgo needed to see if Gangsta Slim approved the plan before he agreed or disagreed with the outsiders. Uncle Louta was the chief but here and now Gangsta Slim had to give him the green light before Risgo could make the decision.

His cell phone rang, "Hello?" He answered.

"Get out now! The agents are on their way to surround the resort," Uncle Louta said, "Go, Go, Go. You don't have time to ask questions."

Gangsta Slim disconnected their long-distance call. "Risgo, call Toshiba and tell her to get here now. Code Red." He phoned Mr. Kibble who he'd put up in a safe community, thanks to Uncle Louta's connection.

"Mr. Kibble, I need your eyes in the sky. I need you to hack into the camera system. I need to be able to see everything the camera sees.

"Anything for you my dearest friend." Mr. Kibble replied quickly getting work.

"FBI Agents coming to surround the resort I am in; I need you to work fast."

"In three minutes, sir, you'll be able to see every move they make. You'll be able to see ants crawling on the ground," Mr. Kibble assured him as Gangsta Slim disconnected the line because time was most definitely ticking.

Toshiba was in the room with Mr. Lover Man when Risgo alerted her. She flew up to their suite. Gangsta Slim had already pulled the rug back where he'd actually traced Risgo's feet the very first day they stepped foot into the resort. Risgo raced from the closet with his cable gun.

"Toshiba, get the bars and pulleys." Risgo shouted from over his shoulder.

"How many?"

"Four, cause it's only four of us," Risgo replied as he was standing in his old footprints.

Faydra got the pulley from Toshiba because Toshiba did not have a clue on how to connect it to the cable as her and Risgo, Gangsta Slim watched on his touchscreen as the agents and other local law enforcers sped up to their resort and jumped out of their cars. There were too many to try to count as they were rushing and pouring into the building. No less than a hundred came out to show their support.

Mr. Kibble and Uncle Louta watched as well from their location on their screens. Gangsta Slim had Mr. Kibble on a loudspeaker, "Mr. Kibble.".

"Yes Pal?"

"You pulled up the blueprint of the building?"

"Yes."

"How bout this area?" Gangsta Slim asked.

"I'm on top of things now, as we speak."

Risgo stood five feet away from their side of the building window. He aimed directly into the resort building window which was half the length of a football field away. He pulled the trigger; the arrow went sailing through the air along with the trail of the street's cable. Lagonda and Nifitinma's heart almost jumped out of their chest as the arrow exploded through their room windowpane. Risgo was a couple inches off from his previous target. Lagonda began to panic because now she knew trouble had arrived. She was new to this and not like the Career Criminals and Ridaz. They were true to it. Nifitinma hopped to her task by grabbing the ax from underneath the bed and chopping away at the window pain.

Toshiba attached her crossbar to the cable, Faydra connected the pulley. Risgo helped Toshiba keep her balance as she stood in the windowsill. She looked down and could see police everywhere running back and forth. It was a 75-foot drop and Toshiba was afraid of heights.

"Bitch don't get scared now," Faydra encouraged.

"Toshiba stop looking down and zip ya ass on across," Risgo said.

"We don't have time for pouting," Gangsta Slim added.

"Bye bitch," Faydra said as she gave Toshiba a hard shove.

Toshiba closed her eyes tight and held her breath as long as she could while traveling toward Nifitinma and Lagonda's room. By the time Toshiba was halfway across, Faydra had on her gloves and her crossbar attached to the cable. She was standing in the windowsill, gripping the attached bar as if she was patting the gas on a motorcycle.

"I'll see y'all on the other side," she said and took flight across the cable like a little kid having fun.

Being in danger never crossed her mind because danger was her second nature. She was definitely Risgo's ride or die chick and was down from day one. Bonnie and Clyde did not have shit on those two.

"The Narcs are about four more floors away from you guys," Mr. Kibble reported from his table.

"Risgo, go," Gangsta Slim commanded before Risgo had the opportunity to become the great debater. Gangsta Slim always goes last; keeping himself in harm's way to make sure they are safe and out of harm's way.

Risgo followed the instructions because there wasn't any time to waste arguing. The sooner he was halfway across, the sooner Gangsta Slim could follow suite.

"Sir, there's a shop on your left soon as you flee from the building and it rents out scuba-gear. Go scuba-diving and lay low on the bottom of the ocean with the fish. A half hour to an hour the cruise ship will arrive, and you Americans will blend in beautifully with the American tourist," Mr. Kibble advised.

"Kibble, I'll see you soon" Gangsta Slim said as he pushed off the windowsill, trying to catch up with Risgo before he reached the other side, which was truly impossible but that did not stop Gangsta Slim from trying.

The agents kicked in six wrong doors before they finally reached their correct destination. They completely wasted all that manpower because they came up empty handed. In their minds and hearts, it was impossible for the crew to escape, but they learned today that nothing was impossible. One of the agents whispered to another, and it truly hurt his heart to admit, but "This crew must be the mission impossible. They were always one step ahead of us, like they could feel when we were coming or smell us like Americans do the rain."

"We would have made history today," the other agent said as he studied how well the cable was secured into the resort wall.

"These guys, they are the best of the best."

"I bet'cha they were trained by the best," the other agent said, "the only way they'll get caught is if they want to get caught and it'll be a trick to it."

"They're in the top ten of America's Most Wanted, so they cannot continue to hide out. Even though for some strange reason I feel they are well connected with Career Criminals all around the world."

***

Agent Narma slammed a closed fist down onto his desk. A good friend and superior of his became the bearer of bad news.

"We came up empty handed."

Narma knew he couldn't get mad at the messenger, "Your guess is as good as mine, but shit does happen."

"Their gotdamn Uncle!" Narma blurred out of frustration.

"You give the retired old man too much credit Narma. Our people probably were slow poking around and that's what happens when we pussy foot around," The Superior said. "I took a look at the old man and he did not look all that smart to me."

"Louta Williams is smarter than he looks." Narma warned as he stared at his boss.

"Jesus," he added and wondered how this guy fell into this

position. If he racked through Uncle Louta's background check with a fine-tooth comb, he learned that the Williams always whoodini'ed their way up out of shit and the tracks started with the so-called old man. The Superior began," the old man's not playing hide-n-go-seek with us. We entrap him. We should be able to get to them."

Agent Narma grew angrier, "Since when have you known a wise old fox to get caught in a fox trap that's been set? Please explain to me how that bullshit happens."

"Shit does happen, and I'm a living witness."

Narma could see this conversation wasn't going anywhere so he excused himself from the Top Dawg's presence. He needed to be in the company of Reese and Pete because they all spoke the same language. His superior was on the high horse and didn't have to think. He got paid as well as got the credit for agents under him.

"Louta was a muthafucka in his prime and now he's even wiser and show nuff is a muthafucka, Narma thought as he exited the office and headed to Reese's office.

CHAPTER 12

Two days later the crew walked around the tourist area. Gangsta Slim and Risgo wore fake beards, sunshades, and fitted caps. Faydra, Nifitinma, Toshiba, and Lagonda wore wigs and sunglasses. Every small shop they passed sold some type of souvenir items. The salesperson was only wasting their sales pitch with them because making a purchase wasn't their interest. They were out and about because being cooped up for a day was enough rest. Gangsta Slim wanted to keep it moving in order to kill the day. Besides, what good would it be to be on vacation and not enjoy it.

Toshiba wanted to go into one of the bars that was several feet away. Gangsta Slim saw her eyeing one and stated, "there will be no drinking today."

Last night he did not protest the girls smoking weed. Toshiba, Faydra and Nifitinma had put smoke into the air since they proclaimed it calmed their nerves. Toshiba had been underneath her little brother's wings for so long she acted like D.B.. She wasn't like Faydra or Nifitinma, she could care less if Gangsta Slim approved. Majority of the time she did what she wanted, when she wanted, and as much as she wanted.

Risgo had to tell her that Slim wasn't out to control nor babysit her. He's only out to protect her and keep her out of harm's way. Toshiba came back with; she was grown and could take care of her damn self.

Her and Slim stayed bumping heads. When Faydra and Nifitinma gets in her business, by encouraging her to listen to Gangsta Slim, because he did have her best interest at heart, she would go off on them, saying fuck him and y'all. In her mind if he tried to steer her right, she would go left.

Gangsta Slim sensed some tension growing between him and first cousin. Rather than feed into it, he suggested they all get massages and chill by the Jacuzzi. Everyone was on edge and needed to release some tension and stress one way or another.

The Ridaz got a little tipsy thanks to Toshiba. Lagonda wanted to decline, she didn't give a damn about Toshiba hollering about being a party pooper. The shit Toshiba was trying to tell her went into one ear and out the other. Especially when she continued barking that bullshit about how Gangsta Slim controlled her life. Gangsta Slim whispered in his wife's ear to join the girls, so his first cousin would shut the fuck up. He just wanted to lay back and allow the boiling water to assist him to foresee their situation crystal clear. Every time Gangsta Slim closed his eyes it was like he was looking into a crystal-ball, seeing into the future, seeing beyond déjà vu.

Risgo respected the tranquility Gangsta Slim had behind his eyelids. He did not see how he was able to block Toshiba's big ass mouth out. Toshiba talks like she is a leader but doesn't have a single follower.

"I'm hungry," Toshiba blurted because her stomach

growled.

"We all are," Gangsta Slim replied, "We'll eat a little later," He needed to check on a few more things.

He had a hunch that was riding him like a spirit.

Their breakfast consisted of fruits and cheeses. Gangsta Slim did not want them to get full because the side-effects would be lazy, tired, and sleepy. Toshiba thought he always had something to say and with Gangsta Slim the feeling was mutual.

Gangsta Slim focused on their safety. The heat, water, or food did not distract him. He looked at the people in passing as if they were ghosts. Behind his dark shades his eyes swept the area. Gangsta Slim doesn't become paranoid, Uncle Louta trained him to always be cautious. His instincts were one hundred percent accurate as he felt the eight pairs of eyes on them.

The four agents were too sloppy. The female that followed them, he remembered seeing her twice back at the resort they escaped from in the nick-of-time. The guy on the right a mile away gave himself away by looking in their direction three times straight. Now the one on their left, posted behind a souvenir book stand did extremely too much. He was sneak talking and mumbling into his blue-tooth earpiece, plus both of his hands were in the pockets of his hoodie. The Jamaican man made the ultimate mistake by standing on the bar porch too long. He did not have a drink in his hands and behind his shades he stared at them the whole time they were on the strip.

Gangsta Slim's eyes recorded their surroundings and allowed him to revisit the screen in his mind, as if he was actually watching TV, or a movie.

"Y'all hold up a minute," Gangsta Slim commanded as the other tourist people continued to walk back and forth of them.

"Hold up for what?" Toshiba asked.

"Because he said so!" Risgo said.

Toshiba rolled her eyes. She never back talked nor challenged Risgo. She had some kind of personal vendetta with Gangsta--Slim for some strange reason.

"Baby, what's wrong?" Lagonda asked as she walked close to Gangsta Slim.

She knew her man like the back of her hand. The panic in her voice caused Gangsta--Slim not to delay their situation.

"Risgo and Faydra," Gangsta Slim addressed because what he had in mind Toshiba or Nifitinma did not have the skills to successfully complete. "Lagonda, Toshiba, and Nifitinma," He continued, "Y'all don't look around. Don't do anything unnatural. There's no reason to panic."

"Where are they Cuz?" Risgo asked.

"As of now to my knowledge, we have four of them on our asses and I'm pretty damn sure they're gonna have us surrounded any minute now," Gangsta Slim said.

"Over my dead body," Faydra said but still keeping her composure.

"We can take out four and make a run for it," Gangsta Slim said.

Risgo kneeled faking like he was tying his shoe and Gangsta Slim informed him of the two agents up ahead that he needed to take out since he was the best shooter. Faydra pulled out a blunt and fired it up as she peeked over at her target.

"Here Ridaz," Faydra stuck to her and her crew's tradition before it's time to kill or be killed.

Toshiba accepted the blunt, taking a long drag and while exhaling the smoke she also released. "Blaze and Glory! No muthafuckin worries."

After Nifitinma got her a good hit of the blunt, she stated, "I was born ready."

Lagonda could not wait to get her hands on the blunt, to wrap her lips around it, to fill her lungs with smoke, giving the butterflies in her stomach something to fight with.

"Faydra, you can't miss," Risgo told the love of his life.

"That's a woman's name," Faydra replied as she took the blunt from Lagonda and got one more puff before dropping it on the ground and stepping on it.

"Do anyone have on anything they brought here?" Gangsta Slim asked, "Clothes or jewelry?"

"Earrings, watch, bracelets! Nothing?" Risgo re-asked.

Toshiba felt embarrassed for what she had to do, but it had to be done. She dug down in the front of her pants and was successful with removing the circle shaped earring from her clit. She had not worn panties since the night Mr. Lover man pierced her most private part.

"I did Slim," Toshiba said, "here," and dropped it in the palm of his hand.

Gangsta Slim instructed everyone to form a small circle facing him, so the agents wouldn't be able to see their hands. In the baby huddle, he withdrew his two pistols and instructed Faydra and Risgo to brandish their weapons as well.

"Risgo, get in position so when we all spin around, we'll be able to hit our targets. They wouldn't expect us to bring them a gun fight out in the open. Especially amongst this crowd of bystanders. They'll hesitate to fire until they can get a clear shot at us. We have the advantage over them. Let's take full benefit of it."

"Faydra, you ready?" Risgo asked.

"I stay ready to keep from having to get ready," she spit verbatim the sentence he had taught her.

Nifitinma felt jealous because she wasn't blessed with the opportunity to do some gangsta shit with D.B. before he went back home to the creator.

"Toshiba?" Gangsta Slim called out because he wanted to get her attention.

Toshiba had her head down, she felt guilty for not listening to him in the first place, "Yeah, big cuz? I'm listening."

"I need for you and Nifitinma to get my baby to safety. Y'all don't need to draw y'all's weapons because as long as they can see y'all empty hands - y'all ain't a threat. So, when we start busting y'all haul ass to a car and call Unk! He'll have our safety net to pick y'all up and we'll catch up soon as we can," Gangsta Slim said.

"Big cuz, I love you,"

"Toshiba, I love you too."

"Slim, anything you need me to do?" Nifitinma asked.

"Take care of Lagonda and Toshiba for me and don't let me down."

"I won't!!" Nifitinma promised. She was going to guard them with her life without question. She wanted to be more active with Gangsta Slim here and now.

"Faydra?"

"What's up, G"

"You ready?"

"I'm a certified Ridaz 'til I diz-zzy."

"Risgo, you ready to jump this bitch off?"

"Say the word, Bru," Risgo said as he gripped his handgun.

"Then let's give these pigs what they looking for since they've chosen death," Gangsta said.

He stole a quick kiss from Lagonda and sped away from his loved ones. Racing in the direction of the agent who blocked their path.

Lagonda, Toshiba, and Nifitinma followed a short distance behind Gangsta Slim as if he was their blocker and one of them was running a football. They piled in the back seat of the first Uber in sight as Gangsta Slim continued racing through the crowd. The agent on his list did not see death coming. He was too busy looking at an incoming call on his phone. Gangsta Slim put six slugs into his chest, the agent's vest material wasn't any match for the cop killer bullets.

As soon as he spun around, Risgo gave both of his victim's head shots. Uncle Louta taught him how to throw a can into the air and shoot the moving object no less than six or seven times before it hit the ground. He shared all his knowledge with Faydra so they would be equal. The female agent was a piece of cake for Faydra. She was not expecting a gun fight amongst the tourists, afraid of accidentally hitting somebody's child, wife, or husband in the process all four agents lost their lives.

Gangsta Slim flipped over the rail and landed on the beach. He continued running through the sand and people. There were children by the ocean feeding the dolphins. He sprinted into their direction as his plan began to come together. He stopped by a little girl and her mother as they were feeding a dolphin a tuna fish, "you from the states, ne bo?" the Jamaican woman asked Gangsta Slim as her eyes undressed his sexy American ass.

"I'm afraid to say I am," he answered and asked "do you mind if I feed the dolphin one of your fish? I never fed a dolphin before in my life."

"Rudy Boi, you can feed me cause I want to feed you," she flirted. Gangsta Slim threw the fish in the dolphin's mouth and sprinted off towards the Jamaican teens that played around on their rented jet-skies.

CHAPTER 13

C.I.A., F.B.I., and Navy Seals traveled by jet-skies, speedboats, and a helicopter. They knew Gangsta Slim rode the jet ski into the ocean. The tracking device indicated he's within two miles of them. The helicopter stopped in the area their GPS located. The agents in the boat wore scuba diving gear and over a dozen of them jumped into the water.

"He won't get away this time," the agent in charge announced.

Agents Narma, Pete, and Reese sat in their comfortable room watching everything on the TV screen but talked straight to the agent from Narma's speaker phone.

"His bullshit bout to come to an end," Narma said.

"Every dog has his day," Pete said, as he removed the unlit cigarette from his mouth.

"I wish it could be us getting his ass," Reese said.

"The son-of-bitch killed four of our agents," The head man reported. "Who would have thought they would start a gun fight in the midst of over a thousand tourist?"

"They do shit you wouldn't think they'll do," Narma alerted, "They're animals. They have no regards for human life."

"They have no regard for life period," Pete added.

"Boss, Boss," one of the scuba-divers radioed in.

"Come in, I'm here," the commander breathed into his walky-talky.

"Boss, the GPS is a dolphin. Somehow, one way or another the guy got smart and fed it to one of the dolphins," The scuba-diver reported. He felt offended by being outsmarted. He actually felt more stupid than he looked. "We been on a ghost mission the entire time."

"Damn it," the commander snapped, "Bullshit!"

"Jesus," Narma sprung out of his chair. He used the remote to cut the TV off and pushed the end button to disconnect his line with the commander.

"Unfucking believable," Reese said.

"He took the tracking device off the girl and fed it to the dolphin. So, our people have been following the fucking dolphin all of this time," Pete said, as he dropped down into a chair to take a load off.

Narma told them from this day forward don't take any chances and to kill the Williams on sight. He did not give a fuck if it was in cold blood. There was not any room for hesitation because they are not going to hesitate for one bit. One second, one minute of hesitation is too damn long. If these people see any weaknesses, our team will be doomed. They'll use anything and everything to their advantage.

Please don't underestimate these people for the sake of your wives and kids. These guys live by the motto, they rather be judged by twelve than carried by six.

The four agents forgot all about the warning, as well as their training when the Williams turned a smooth day into a life and death situation. Narma knew why their agents came up with the short end of the stick. People are good for saying what they would do until they get caught in the situation. Trying to push them Career Criminals right and they'll fight like hell to continue stepping left.

"I never thought these type of people existed until I took this oath," Reese said as he paced around the room with both hands behind his back.

"Welcome to the club," Narma agreed.

Pete toyed with the unlit cigarette and snatched it out of his mouth once again, "They are impossible to figure out. We always think we got one of them and then we come out empty handed. Now I honest to God think I'm ready to try hoping in one fucking hand and taking a fucking shit in the other one to actually see which one is gonna fill the fuck up first."

Narma sat in his seat, "When you do your shitting method, please do it on your own time." and he went on to tell them what their director thought. "We need to focus on digging up some evidence on Louta, so we can take him down. Once we kill the head the body will follow. They will be clueless without the old man."

"Good luck," Reese said as he looked into Narma's direction, "How long we been trying that bright idea?"

This type of language was music to Pete's ears. A beautiful and crooked smile kissed him on the lips. He did not hear another word that came out of his partners mouth because he was in another world. One that only the people inside would understand. Outsiders would probably have a heart-attack or be mentally destroyed if not commit suicide because sometimes somethings not good for the goose, as it is for the gander.

One time or another the sun will shine on a dog's ass, Pete thought as he gummed away on the unlit cigarette. *There's always a first time for everything.*

CHAPTER 14

Gangsta Slim and Risgo had tracked down agent Ivory along with a little inside assistance. He had not been with the Bureau long enough to learn how to make himself invisible. They disguised themselves again and when they rode by his house, there was Toshiba, parked a couple houses away. She had overheard them talking about not leaving until they caught Ivory for what he had done to her.

Gangsta Slim called her phone as Risgo parked their stolen Pet Control white van a street over and behind Toshiba's black SUV truck.

"Toshiba, what the fuck you think you doing?" Gangsta Slim went off, "The shit you doing is not smart, it's a suicide mission!"

"I'm doing what us Williams do."

"Girl, don't give me that bullshit, now get the fuck on back to the hotel, where the girls are at and allow me and Risgo to finish what we started."

Toshiba wiped a few tears off her face, "I put y'all in jeopardy and you been risking your life for me long enough. I can handle this muthafucka."

Risgo was wise enough to know that trying to talk some sense into Toshiba was like whipping a dead horse. Once a Williams makes up their mind to do something all you can do is buckle the fuck up and try to enjoy the ride.

"Yo T, we parked behind you. We got ya back if shit doesn't go according to plan," Risgo said, "You get the fuck out of dodge."

"OK, big cuz."

"T, there's a place two blocks over where they do parachute jumping. Nifitinma is waiting on us there. If possible, get him there and we'll do the rest," Risgo said as he gripped the steel wheel, but wished it was one of Toshiba's arms since she is trying to steal their show.

As soon as they disconnected lines Ivory came cruising down the street in his vehicle. He parked in the gate of his house. Toshiba eased up to his curb and called out his name. Ivory looked like he had seen a ghost. He rushed over to her truck fearing his wife would come to the front door. She just had their newborn son. Ivory had to get Toshiba far away from here. He did not want to put his family life at stake.

He climbed into the passenger seat, "What are you doing here?" He asked.

Toshiba pulled away from the curb without asking for his approval, "I miss that big ass dick. I want to suck it and fuck it before I leave the country."

Ivory thought totally no different. He thought I might as well get me some more of this fire ass head and bomb ass pussy before this bitch goes six feet deep. As Toshiba drove, he was lost in lust until they reached the parachute jump location.

"You jump?" he asked.

"I love the thrill," she replied, in a sexy voice.

Once they got out of the truck, Lagonda met them, faking like she was an employee, both female employees had been hogtied and placed in a closet ass naked - they needed their uniforms for the plan to work. Faydra and Nifitinma had the pilot's co-workers duct taped. Faydra explained the importance to the pilot, of her and her girl's safety was absolutely up to her, so she better not try any tricks.

"Bitch fly this bitch right," Nifitinma warned as she poked the pilot in her jaw with the pistol, letting her get a very good feel of the steel. Ivory and Toshiba walked over as Lagonda lead the way, "all-a-board," Faydra said as Gangsta Slim and Risgo pulled up. Ivory knew he was outnumbered as well as had to reap the consequences without it trickling down to his wife and child. Especially since Toshiba was feet away from his doorstep.

"What would you have done if I would've gone in my house and not came back out to you?" Ivory couldn't rest until he got the question off of his mind.

"I would have burned that bitch to the ground and everybody who was in it. Your old ass sick ma'am, baby's momma, and the infant," Toshiba said.

Gangsta Slim and Risgo escorted everyone inside the plane as Ivory continued his conversation with Toshiba.

"I thought y'all would be at-least halfway out of the country by now."

"See, us Williams is a different type of species," Toshiba cocked her head sideways, "We'll do the opposite of what you would think we would do. I know good damn well they don't pay you to think," Toshiba displayed a fake smile, "you actually thought I would allow you to get away scott free? I'm a ride or die bitch! It gets my nipples and clit hard when I take risks."

Risgo and Gangsta Slim said to themselves, "Toshiba has been around doing so damn much she began to think like him, talk like him, and do insane shit like him. D.B. turned her the fuck out, into a cold-blooded psychopath."

This bitch got balls, Ivory thought, as well as by him been a toenail away from death caused his morning breakfast to rush back up his throat. He vomited on Toshiba.

"You filthy pig," Toshiba said and rushed into the corner to change into a jump-suit.

Ivory studied the notorious group of killers. No-one looked dangerous but Gangsta Slim and Nifitinma. The rest of them did not look like they had a dangerous bone in their bodies. He read and re-read over their cases. The Career-Criminals, two-man gang; Risgo and Gangsta Slim did not care about tomorrow. Lagonda did not fit the characteristics of a Ridaz. Her face showed up nowhere in their bureau. If possible, she would be the one Ivory would try if the opportunity presented itself.

Risgo's watch began to beep as him and Gangsta Slim sat by the jump out area. Risgo got up and stepped into his jumpsuit and slipped his parachute back on in one swift motion. After words he threw one by Ivory's feet, instructing him to do the same. Ivory watched Gangsta Slim the whole time. Gangsta Slim blinked an eye not once, the man kept a stone face and said not a word. Gangsta Slim suited-up behind him. Risgo looked at his watch and down towards the ground, which was all lakes.

"Our jump is coming up," Risgo announced.

Lagonda walked over, kissing, and hugging Gangsta Slim, which explained to Ivory why she was among the group. Ivory couldn't hear what she whispered to him over the rustling airplane noise. Faydra did the same with Risgo.

She walked out of her lover's arms and went straight to Ivory, putting her pistol to his temple while grabbing a fist full of his collar, "Bitch, Muthafucka, you try any fucking thing stupid I'll scatter your fucking brains all over this fucking plane."

"That what the fuck I need to be doing," Toshiba said.

Nifitinma just stared at him, sending mental death threats until he briefly stared back making her feel uncomfortable.

Nifitinma walked up to him, "Pussy Nigga, why the fuck you staring at me? You sizing me the fuck up? You thinking I'm the bitch for you to try?"

"No Ma'am," Ivory said.

His eyes finally got him in trouble, and it wasn't for looking at ass or pussy. The woman punked him out as if he was a pussy.

"Go cuz," Risgo said to Gangsta Slim.

Gangsta Slim stepped off the plane with his legs and arms open wide. He fought and protested against the wind. The two-hundred-foot fall gave him one hell-of-a rush because he was afraid of heights, but always set out to conquer his fears.

Risgo jumped two minutes behind him but in a diving style, which allowed his body to penetrate through the wind as if he was a bullet while his hands rested on both sides of his body. Faydra started her sixty second count and on the dot, and she escorted Ivory over because it was his turn.

"Bitch, see ya and don't wanna be ya," Toshiba said to him.

In his mind he said, *Bitch please. I should've murdered you after I fucked you.*

"Get the fuck off the plane bitch," Faydra said.

Nifitinma kicked him in the ass causing him to tumble and sail against the wind which made the crew's plan even sweeter. Toshiba wanted to use Ivory's body as target practice but feared one of her bullets could go astray and hit Gangsta Slim or Risgo, so she stuck to the script like Gangsta Slim always lectured her to.

Risgo was flying and speeding through the air like superman. Once he was able to grab Gangsta Slim's back-pack Risgo twisted his body, so he was able to lay on Gangsta Slim's back and draw his pistol as if he was in a drawing contest. Three bullets escaped his barrel catching agent Ivory twice in the forehead and once between the eyes. The first shot killed him, the other two were for good measures.

Risgo coached Gangsta Slim to pull the cord so his parachute would open. They would rather be early than late because all of the lakes and ponds underneath them were filled with alligators and crocodiles. The extra twenty-five feet gave them more time to maneuver so the wind would guide them to safety.

They witnessed the sixteen to twenty-one feet long creatures swimming around. Normally all of the body that they did not eat would be stored or buried until they were ready to finish it off, but here and now there was a lot of mouths that needed to be fed, so the body did not stand a chance once it hit the water.

As Gangsta Slim and Risgo were growing closer to the

ground they saw twenty-five deep armed Mexicans, not one of them spoke or understood any English. Their guns would spit out no less than a hundred rounds before one could even think about breathing.

The leader began saying something in Spanish. Twenty of the guys raced to the area Risgo and Gangsta Slim would soon be landing. The Mexican bullets were in a hundred round plastic cover to keep from getting damaged or rearranged as they dragged the ground. Two more jeeps pulled up and Mexicans jumped out with razor sharp machetes which they used to cut off heads and other body parts. These guys played no games; death would not escape them.

Twelve minutes later Gangsta Slim and Risgo were escorted on foot to a seven-acre compound. There were plenty baby Beyoncé's and many sexy J-Lo's as cooks, maids, and servants. A short fat Mexican with a curly afro, full well-groomed beard, and hairy chest stood before them.

Risgo mumbled to Gangsta Slim, "That's the Maiseyon."

"The what?"

"The rich muthafucka who runs this shit. He's a drug lord," Risgo continued to mumble and whisper.

"Come, Come. My friends," The Maiseyon welcomed.

This room was exquisite with expensive furniture. The building could be considered a small palace; there were ten armed guards at an arm's length of The Maiseyon.

Risgo stepped forward and Gangsta Slim did the same. The Maiseyon shook both of their hands while he still had Gangsta Slim embraced, he said, "My friend, I have heard a lot of great things about you. I'm glad that we finally could meet."

"We would've been here a couple days earlier, but we had

some unfinished business t to tend to," Risgo said.

"Why didn't you ask for assistance?" The Maiseyon asked, "it would have been my pleasure to assist you."

"Sometimes we like to get our own hands dirty," Risgo said with a wink. He knew exactly the kind of work The Maiseyon was talking about because that was the term him and his people used for murder.

"So why your soldiers don't speak English?" Gangsta Slim asked.

"I don't need my field soldiers to do any kind of communicating- that's my job. But many of them here at my compound speak it fluently. Would you gentlemen like food and wine?"

"Some other time," Gangsta Slim said, "actually we would like to run in and run out."

"Drop in and drop out would be more like it," The Maiseyon said, laughing, but he liked guys who liked to get straight to business. "I was told you was the man who could take care of what I need taken care of," The Maiseyon said Risgo, since that's where he'd gathered his information from their first day of meeting.

"As long as you can cover our fee, anything is possible," Gangsta Slim assured.

The Maiseyon laid a hand on Gangsta Slim's shoulder, "My friend this is not an easy task because if it was so simple me and my men wouldn't be in need of your services. What makes you think you're going to be so successful?" He looked Gangsta Slim deep into the eyes, Gangsta Slim did not bat an eye.

"Did you think Evil Knievel was going to be successful

when he first tried to jump the Grand Canyon before the world on national TV?" Gangsta Slim asked. "The man believed in himself! He was willing to lose his life trying. Think about all the risk-taking events he experienced before he went to that big step?"

The Maiseyon looked over to Risgo, surprised at the response he received. He began to laugh and pat Gangsta Slim on the shoulder a couple times and said, "My friend, I love this guy."

"What price you have in mind?" Gangsta Slim cut to the chase.

"It's five of y'all. I'll give you each five million." the Maiseyon offered.

Gangsta Slim held up six fingers. Risgo did not add Yan Kibble to the equation, he was not going to leave him out. "It's six of us and we'll take ten million each."

There was nothing to negotiate or ponder, the Maiseyon needed them to agree to do the job no one else was foolish or brave enough to complete. So, the Maiseyon lived up to his name by going up two more notches.

"My friend, my money comes free so I'll give each one of you 12 million apiece and if you can get the job done within seven days. I'll give you eight million more as a bonus."

The Maiseyon was a smart man. He threw out numbers they could not refuse. Besides, in his mind the whole time he was planning on giving them 20 million apiece, which wasn't close to the profit he made in a month. A hundred million wouldn't be the dust off his money. When the price is right, a man will try to move a mountain or die trying.

CHAPTER 15

Uncle Louta decided today would be a day as ever to take a ride through the streets. Every now and then he liked to make himself available and show the people that he was very much approachable. People would tell him their problems. Uncle Louta began to light up instead of tightening up. The conversation would end with them saying," Mr. Williams, you are a reasonable man and thank you for hearing me out." Uncle Louta wasn't getting soft. He actually was coming to his senses. In reality, he needed the people. They would help him do all of his dirty work and sometimes looked for nothing in return, But Uncle Louta was wise enough to acknowledge a favor as a favor and never left owing anyone.

When Uncle Louta used to play hard ball with them, he always came out with the long end of the stick. They still respected him and stayed loyal to him. They knew from experience he was ruthless and knew it was better to be with him than against him. Their sea-saw relationship kept them both afloat. They took the good with the bad.

It hurt Uncle Louta to his heart every time he passed by the condemned building. There was nothing like enjoying a plate of Crumbwell's Barbecue. From time to time he would send one of his nephews in town to get them a hundred dollars' worth, even though he could barbecue his ass off. Mr. and Mrs. Crumbwell's been in business for over forty years. Once they became old and ill, they passed the business down to their four adult children who weren't able to see, nor understand the phrase, business was business.

He cruised through the hoods as well. Knowing that someday some of them little bad ass boys are going to get their families out of the ghetto and put their mothers into houses, as well learn to do things to make her proud, and to become the opposite of him and his family occupation.

Upon seeing the kids huddled in front of a pinky-dinky truck, he rode his brakes to a halt, parking behind the ice cream truck. He got out and left his car running and excused himself through the crowd until he reached the truck window.

When he got the driver's attention, Uncle Louta handed him two, one hundred-dollar bills, "Son, this should be more than enough for all of these kids out here to get whatever they want. Continue to go through the hood giving out free Ice Cream until the two bills are gone."

"Thank you, sir," the driver replied, "and for your concern for the kids, I'm going to match ya generosity."

"By wholesale price or by your regular sale price?" Uncle Louta asked, smiling. He began working his way back through the mob of kids. He missed it when the pinky-dinky man saluted him.

Uncle Louta walked over to the biggest kid, especially since he looked like a bully and had the size of one. The fourteen-year-old looked up at him through large Teddy-Bear eyes and wondered why this strange old man was coming his direction. He began to question himself; has he stolen something, or took one of them little boys' money today? Was it behind him slapping a girl in school last week? Uncle Louta put his young curious mind to rest.

"Son, I need you to do me a favor?" Uncle Louta said.

"What? Fo what?" the fourteen-year-old asked. The scared little boy voice could not go unnoticed.

Uncle Louta's presence alone humbled the baby giant.

"Lil homie, I need for you to keep the other lil homies in line and don't let them get into trouble. Son, trouble is easy to get into and hard as hell to get out of. It took my dumb ass forty long and hard years to learn that." Uncle Louta pulled out five twenty-dollar bills and a hundred-dollar bill. He knew this would catch the young buck's undivided attention.

He held the five twenties in one hand and the hundred-dollar bill in the other hand and asked, "Which one you want?"

The baby giant pointed to the five twenties, "That one! I want the one that will make a bank roll."

Uncle Louta granted his wish as well as shook that dog finger at him, "yo lil ass better keep them outta trouble cause if you don't Imma come and see bout ya."

Uncle Louta used the term homie, so that he'll be speaking the child's language. He held up the money because that's a way to capture the youth's attention. When you talking about the Benjamin's - people will listen.

The baby giant thumbed through the money and said to himself, "You can learn a lot from a dummy and that's not to be one."

Uncle Louta jumped back into his ride. He was ready to get

back to his neck of the woods. After bending a corner or two he crossed paths with a group of hustlers. There was one who stuck out like a sore thumb, PK junior was Polo'd down from head to toe. The eighteen-year-old looked like his father spat him out. Uncle Louta nodded sadly as he laid eyes on the platinum necklace and cross JR wore. It was all his mother had that could make her son feel some kind of connection to PK.

She told PK that she was pregnant and needed extra money. He told her that he would bring her two thousand dollars back that night. She said, "give me that necklace and if ya ass don't come back, Imma pawn this bitch."

PK got murdered before he could make it back. PK's son's mother was a prostitute, an old ho and that's all she knew. PK gave her mother a pound of weed and the old lady did not look back. Grandma made PK Junior a certified trap star. They had their turf on lock. Uncle Louta propositioned the old lady, but she wasn't trying to hear any of it. She wasn't giving up her only grandson. Uncle Louta hollered at the youngsta a few times but by then him and his Granny was smoking weed and grinding together. Granny was his OG, he did not care to mingle with his father's side of the family. They say an old dog can't be taught new tricks; PK Junior's Granny was a living witness. She asked Ciera how to do this and that. All of her schooling came from her phone. Granny didn't finish school, but she could google her ass off.

A hustler noticed Uncle Louta at the stop sign watching them, so he threw up both hands in a gangsta like meaning, "what's up?" which totally put Uncle Louta in the spotlight.

PK Junior looked in his direction and he told his people, "I got this," and he slick walked over to Uncle Louta's vehicle.

"What's the business old man?" he greeted Uncle Louta.

"You been giving it some thought of what I said?"

PK Junior licked his lips, "Unk. I'm the only fam that my Granny have. My momma and her fucking pimp have a long ass bid. She gonna need all the assistance and papers I can shift her way and besides, I can't bail the fuck out and leave my Granny hanging. Family, you feel me Big Dawg."

Uncle Louta nodded, He respected his nephew's mind, "son if you need me for anything give me a holla."

"I feel all of that Big Dawg," PK Junior said as he was taking steps backwards giving Uncle Louta a clear sign that his little five minutes of fame was over.

"Son?"

"Speak ya peace, I'm listening Unk?"

"I know that hustla shit in ya DNA because ya father liked slanging that weed shit."

PK Junior started jumping around while playfully slapping himself on the wrist with two fingers, "You say Pop liked slanging it, but I love it I run that checkup."

Uncle Louta gripped the steering wheel, "Son be safe."

"Big Dawg, I'm aware of the shit that comes with the territory. I'm a Risk Taker."

Uncle Louta could not get mad no matter how much he tried or wanted to. He had to respect his great-nephew's gangster. PK Junior inherited and incorporated PK's passion.

When Uncle Louta made it to the bottom of his mile-long dirt road it did his heart good to see Keisword Jr had his brothers and first cousin out in the woods training. Uncle Louta always preached, the fox had to set the trap for the other foxes or in other words stay ready to keep from having to get ready.

The one who is a step ahead will win. Keisword Jr and his brothers held up a few foxes apiece. D.B. Jr. had three by the feet in each hand and two more thrown across his shoulder. Uncle Louta smiled and winked at him, which was a waste of time and energy because they could not see him behind the tinted windows.

CHAPTER 16

Since Pete graduated from agent to special agent, he learned how to use the bureau to his advantage, and by him being able to go into the evidence room as he pleases. Pete would hide things underneath their noses and put things clear in their faces and the other law-enforcers wouldn't have a clue.

Pete swiped his card and the steel door opened. Once he entered, the door closed and locked behind him. He went straight to the mobile six-foot steel stairs and rolled it to his destination. After climbing to the top and moving around a few boxes and packages he was successful with locating his almost two-decade old package.

Once Pete had wheeled the stairs back to its normal spot, he exited the evidence room with his package. "Damn it," he thought, withholding the information away from Narma and Reese that Narma was going to pitch a bitch. Pete knew he had to prepare for the storm coming. Now was the time and place. Without any further delay Pete went into an unoccupied conference room and placed the tape into the slot that brought the 60-inch screen to life.

He notified Narma and Reese. They entered with their own

special snacks of their choosing. They did not know what to expect. They just blindly came to see what Pete had on his mind.

"I brought you a cup of coffee and a pack of these blueberry donuts" Narma said, as he handed them over to Pete.

"Thank you," Pete said while accepting the southern hospitality.

"So, what's going on in here Pete?" Reese asked.

"Have a seat and I'll show you," Pete said as he placed the donuts on the table and picked up the remote.

"That's what I'm talking about let me see it instead of letting me hear it," Narma joked as he sat in a comfortable chair.

Reese did the same, "A great king once said, why stand when you can sit," he said while crossing his legs and locking his fingers together, resting them by his knees.

Pete aimed the remote at the flat-screen and within seconds he appeared on the screen. When they all were in their places. Narma immediately looked at Reese with a frown. Reese hunched up his shoulders and remained quiet.

He wanted to see what the tape had to offer before he started running off at the mouth. On the video, Pete stood before a girl about twenty-years old. She looked upset and seemed she had been crying her heart out as she was providing information, "Remember the four guys that got killed at the motel?"

"Yes," Pete answered, taking a seat behind the desk immediately switching on the desktop computer.

"My brother and his crew weren't trying to rob the old man for the Chevy. They murdered his nephew PK and that's why the old man murdered them. He called himself getting revenge," she cried and sniffed out on the video.

"The old man took law in his own hands, so he was the judge, jury, and the executioner himself. Is that what you're telling me?"

"Yes," she managed to get out during sniffles.

"How do you know this man?"

"I saw him in the doctor's office when I took my son to get his checkup."

"Mmm," Pete mumbled as he spun the computer around to face Rita, "is this our guy? Is this the guy?

Rita's eyes narrowed, "Yes, he's the killer."

Pete tapped a button on the keyboard Uncle Louta's mugshot vanished and Gangsta Slim and Risgo's mugshots filled the screen.

"You see these guys too?"

"The dark skin slim one."

"How you know him?" Pete asked, studying every inch of Rita's facial expression.

Seems the young girl had aged a decade in the past ten minutes ago.

"He was in the doctor's office with PK," she said and was ready to stop talking before she fucked around and incriminated herself. She wasn't crazy enough to volunteer that she planned the robbery of PK. She had no knowledge they were going to murder PK.

"Sit tight, I will be back in a flash, can I get you anything coffee, cigarettes?"

"No thank you." she moaned and whispered, "Please just get this old bastard who killed my baby daddy."

As soon as he rushed out the door, Pete cut the screen off. "Why did you kill it?" Narma asked.

"Because that was it," Pete said as he placed the remote back on the table and got in gear for the interview that was about to explode.

Questions after questions were going to surface because both of his partners weren't going to harbor them..

"Where you went when you walked out on her?"

"I went to the bathroom Narma."

"Why didn't you notify me?" Narma asked with a voice full of anger. "I was the head man in charge, remember? and I am still!"

"Narma--."

Narma cut Pete's sentence off by saying, "Narma, my ass."

Pete continued, "I analyzed each and every word that came out of her mouth. Once you view the tape you will see she was seeking to get revenge. She altered the story. She added just enough to get our antennas up and deleted what needed to be deleted."

"Pete, even if she did edit the story as you claim, you should have brought it to both of our attention," Reese said as he uncrossed his legs. "Jesus." he exhaled because what he just saw with his two eyes was too much for him to digest.

"Pete, it wasn't your fucking call!" Narma railed off, "It wasn't your call to make the judgement. Why the fuck you did not call us?"

"I told you, she was seeking revenge. We're not the fucking revengers." Pete replied as he began pacing back and forth.

Reese was foaming out the mouth because he couldn't wait to ask Pete this question, even though he already knew the answer to the question, "What became of the girl?"

"I don't know, she left town. She disappeared." Pete said.

"Do you think she just up and vanished? Got ghost? Or was she was wiped clean of the planet?" Reese asked as he stood and gave Pete that look. "Asshole, don't fucking try to bullshit me or play on my fucking intelligence."

"Surely you can't expect us to believe that" Narma stated and asked, "Pete, you don't believe that's what happened ya damn self, now do you?"

"She mentioned Louta's name and Louta killed her in cold blood," Reese predicted as he turned both of his hands into solid fists.

"Louta killed her personally and disposed of her body or he had his nephews to do the dirty work," Narma said.

Pete kept quiet. He only spoke when he was spoken to. He needed them to continue shooting their questions and opinions back and forth to one another. He quietly and quickly excused himself from their presence so they would have the room to get the shit off their chest amongst themselves.

"Reese, I'm telling you, he knows more than what he put out. He is holding back. He is keeping some classified shit away from us."

"Narma, Pete has his shit together. All his lies are in alphabetical order. He's dotted the fucking I's and crossed all the fucking T's as well."

"What does he have to gain by keeping shit from us?" Reese asked.

"What does he have to lose sounds more like it?" Narma answered a question with a question.

Pete spoiled their day and left them with migraines. There was something very, very fishy about Pete's side of the story. Something in the milk wasn't clean. Narma knew it but could not put his finger on it. It was eating him and Reese both alive. Now Reese came to the conclusion that Pete thought his shit didn't stink.

"What's your take of Pete?"

"Reese, right now I don't know what to think," Narma answered as he massaged his temples to relax himself of the headache. "Pete, Pete, Pete" Narma chanted as he continued digging his strong fingertips beside each of his eyes.

"Narma, he's one of us and even if we don't like this situation, we still have to give him the benefit of the doubt." Reese could have saved his breath because Narma had drawn circles around himself. He was in his own world.

***

Pete mentally wrestled with all kinds of notions. His mind would not allow him to rest. He asked himself all kinds of crazy questions and second guessed himself a lot more often. It drove Pete up and down the wall as he wondered what Narma and Reese thought of him. Truly he wanted to call them and see if he could get a good read of their relationship and to see how his credibility stood. Pete wanted to come clean on a lot of things, but some people can't handle the truth. There are some secrets people just have to take to the fuckin grave with them.

Pete's phone rang as he was driving home. He looked at the caller ID and it was Reese. He wanted to answer, but part of his mind told him not to, so he let his voice mail answer.

I'm a got damn coward, Pete whispered to himself then he yelled to a yellow light, "I'm a fucking coward." He reflected over his life and called himself having a solution to his problem by freeing his conscious of the sentence, "I signed the fuck up for this bullshit."

CHAPTER 17

Gangsta Slim and his family set up shop on The Maiseyon's compound. He gave them as much space as needed. The Maiseyon told them "Mi casa es su casa." His soldiers and servers treated them like Kings and Queens. There was no stress underneath The Maiseyon's roof, and they were safe as possible. The more comfortable they got, the better they worked planning and would think more clearly.

Gangsta Slim and Mr. Kibble were in their own room. He did not need any interruptions nor distractions because it was very important that Mr. Kibble say the right words at the right time and play his position because this would be a life or death event.

This would be Mr. Kibble's first rodeo, but for Gangsta Slim, this was his second nature. He breathed, lived, and loved this shit. Now Gangsta Slim had to do something that never has been done before. He had to put his life and freedom in the hands of another man besides Risgo or Uncle Louta.

"Mr. Kibble, Sir, it's easy and simple. You can't deviate from the plan. Not in the slightest way. Sir, all you have to do is stick to my instructions."

"Don't I always," Mr. Kibble said.

This would be a two-way street because both of them had to count on one another and put their life and freedom in one another's hands. But Gangsta Slim has never had to depend on a stranger before.

"My friend, you can count on me," Mr. Kibble said. He saw a look in Gangsta Slim's eyes that he'd never seen before.

"I trust you Mr. Kibble."

"You know I trust you my dear friend," Mr. Kibble said as he jumped into the air with his short self which he always had to do in order to give Gangsta Slim high-five.

"We been through lots together," Gangsta Slim began, "in a short span. We both always count on one another."

"My dear friend, we are going to live a very good and healthy life together, or we are going to die together. I do not fear death," Mr. Kibble stated, "Must I remind you; I was building missiles and one wrong move, one wrong wire...." Mr. Kibble paused to bring his small palms together and separate them at a very fast pace, "goes Ka-Boom." Mr. Kibble exhaled.

"You the man, Mr. Kibble. You the man," Gangsta Slim said, smiling. Now he was one-hundred percent comfortable with himself, which he needed to be, because nothing would come out right when people do things under pressure.

Mr. Kibble knew nothing other than to be a team player and Gangsta Slim made him feel good about himself. This was a new feeling because all Mr. Kibble ever knew was to be on the butt end of someone's joke.

"You the Gangsta," Mr. Kibble said laughing. He did not know Gangsta Slim' name because everyone called him Slim.

He nicknamed Gangsta Slim, Gangsta due to him killing the warhead scientists and to him that was something a gangster would do.

"You the giant," Gangsta Slim said as he began clapping his hands, "You the genius."

As they threw back and forth praises, Mr. Kibble danced around doing the duck walk and his famous chicken dance. Every time he got excited, this would happen, it never failed. Gangsta Slim was the only one who was able to get the child side of Mr. Kibble to come out to play.

***

In the other room Risgo had a map spread across the table. The girls watched in silence as he explained using his trigger finger to skate up and down the large paper map. Faydra always came out being the best student. She was a quick learner. Always paid attention, stayed focused, and simulation brought about stimulation. Her and Risgo have been a couple for over twenty years. They were truly one another's soul mate. She thought and acted just like him. She also took pride in everything she did no matter what it was.

"I gotta go piss," Toshiba said, because to her this was boring, and she needed to find the Mexican who had the weed.

"Bitch get the fuck on," Nifitinma said, in a playful voice, "We don't need to know all of that. That shit too much information."

"Just don't think about ya got damn self," Risgo said, because he was hip to Toshiba's bullshit.

"Yeah, Ms. Selfish," Faydra added.

"I gotta pee too," Lagonda lied because she wanted to follow Toshiba. Plus, she wasn't into what Risgo was talking about. She was greener than grass and in this field, dumber than a box of rocks.

After the baby distraction Faydra got heavy back on Risgo's line. Nifitinma cleared her mind and downloaded every piece of formula Risgo laid out because common sense told her he wasn't talking about this for his health or because he had a mouth. He was talking about this for their best benefit. If they weren't equipped with the tools of knowledge, the girls' asses were going to be out of gas. Nifitinma did not want to rely on Faydra for the instructions or secondhand knowledge. She wasn't like Toshiba. You can lead a horse to the water, but you can't make it drink.

"Say that one more time?" she said, making sure she heard him right the first time. Risgo did not mind repeating himself. By them asking questions proved that he wasn't wasting his time.

"Nifitinma, I need you to know there's no such thing called an elementary question," Risgo began, "the---."

Faydra cut him off and finished the sentence, which he had to explain to her more than once. "the dumbest question is the ones you don't ask, so girl if you don't know or don't understand, stop him and ask. Don't let him go into another subject without getting the first one right."

"That's what the fuck I'm talking bout," Risgo said, as he squeezed Faydra's hand "The student out shined the teacher."

"A bitch gotta be a good student in order to be a good teacher," Nifitinma said, giving Faydra a high-five. She had no problems with giving credit where credit was due.

Risgo took back over the conversation and stressed the importance of their lively-hood and that everyone had a role to play.

"We cannot get to point B if point A isn't right," He paused to look at Nifitinma, "you feel me?"

"Yes."

"See, in order to make shit come out right, we all have to function as if we are one body." Risgo looked at Nifitinma again because she had a mind of her own and will go astray in a heartbeat. She was a hot head. "Nifitinma, the same way y'all count on us, we have to count on y'all. Faydra gonna make sure she instructs y'all how to make shit right." Once Risgo saw she was with him and not against him he drilled Nifitinma's ass.

Risgo had a better rapport with Nifitinma and Toshiba than Gangsta Slim so that's why he made it his responsibility to get deep off in their shit. They were interrupted by a knock on the door. The Spanish accent could be heard when Risgo opened the door.

There were two trucks backing up, "Senor, we have your things."

"Muy bien," Risgo replied in Spanish, which meant 'very good', he did not know much Spanish but learned a little bit of their language from them.

"Buenos Dias," the first Mexican said as Risgo stepped to the side and allowed him to carry the wooden box crate into the room.

"Good morning to you too, amigo," Risgo returned the good morning greeting.

The twenty-five-man group of Mexicans worked like ants

as they stacked the boxes against the wall. When they were finished Risgo said, "Muchos gracias me manos" (Thank you very much my brothers.).

"De nada," (my pleasure) one of them shot back and continued heading back out of the door until he heard Risgo's voice.

"Oo-yee me mano!" (listen my brother.)

The Mexican stopped in his tracks, turning to face Risgo as he whipped sweat out of his face, "Si-Senor?" (Yes sir) "Di-me, amigo." (tell me, I'm listening my friend.)

"Nececito," (I need) Risgo began and paused to put two fingers to his lips expressing him smoking weed; "nececito mota--!"

The Mexican smiled because he understood Risgo was asking for some good weed.

The Mexican replied, "Tran-kilo me amigo, tango para tu en timpo poqito" (Take it easy my friend, I will have it shortly.)

Another Mexican walked over and slapped the Mexican across the head, "Talk English and stop fucking around with these important people, if the boss finds out you over here bullshitting them, he will cut ya fucking head off."

"Homie, I'll be back in a little bit," the Mexican said in English and apologized for bullshitting around like he didn't speak English.

Risgo didn't give a fuck, he just needed to fire up a few blunts to get some of the pressure off of him.

Toshiba and Lagonda came back with a large zip-lock bag of weed. The Maiseyon's main man gave it to them and told them if they needed anything to please don't hesitate to bring it to his attention.

Toshiba wanted to tell him since they exercised for long hours she wanted to see if they could eat pussy good and fuck for long hours. The only thing that stopped her mannish ass was Lagonda's presence. The Mexican wasn't going to decline.

"This pressure good," Risgo admitted after taking the blunt from Toshiba and taking a couple good ass inhales.

"Pressure blow pipes," Faydra added, as she walked up on Risgo and squeezed his dick letting him know how she wanted to relieve her pressure. The way she positioned herself in front of Risgo looked like she was whispering in his ear, no one suspected she was massaging his thick black dick through his pants. Nifitinma got her a hand full of weed and walked towards a table to roll up. Lagonda followed since she's been learning how to roll weed.

"Come on bitch, I'll put ya ass to work," Nifitinma said.

"When it's something I wanna know I ain't got no problem with working," Lagonda said as she tagged along.

Toshiba whispered to Faydra, "I'll stay close to you when the shit takes flight cause I know you gonna tell a bitch what's up."

"That's what's up," Faydra replied.

"Toshiba, you been smoking a lot lately," Risgo pointed out.

"To calm my nerves cuz," Toshiba replied.

"Us being wanted makes a bitch smoke like hell," Nifitinma stated.

"Same shit, different day," Lagonda exercised her voice.

"What y'all expect, we Risk Takers," Risgo explained.

The Mexican that was bullshitting Risgo knocked on the door. Risgo opened the door. He handed Risgo a trash bag full of that pressure, "Special delivery for the Risk Takers," he said in perfect English.

CHAPTER 18

This Pete issue had Narma stressed the fuck out. He was knee deep in ape shit. He stomped around, pouted around, mentally swinging around on branches doing all types of gorilla shit, everything but beating into his chest. Now he had to report to the Regional Director face-to-face because it could not be discussed on the phone. He was responsible and held accountable for Pete and Reese's actions. Their fuck ups were his as well. The girl would still be alive today he thought if he would have learned the situation. He thought about it and decided he was lying to himself, because no-one was safe when Louta Williams wants them out of the picture. As there is a will, there's a way and Louta refused to rest until he destroyed any and everything that can bring harm to him.

Narma reasoned with himself, Louta was a veteran and he somehow always found a way to stay one step ahead of them. His opponents learned from experience not to put anything past Louta nor his family. They all were deadly, dangers, and fearless. They are the type of people that it's impossible to think as they think. They are so unpredictable, and they must be taken down by any means necessary. Trying to catch them was a waste of time and energy. They would have to sacrifice a great deal of law enforcement to do so. His agents had to get on the same band wagon as the Williams to take them down. This meant having to kill or harm any citizens while in the line of duty. The people had to be taken out. They had no problems with bringing some ass to get some ass. This shit is called kill or be killed.

Now Narma began to see the bigger picture. It is better if they were six feet deep than him. Fuck all of that going by the book. In his book, they had no fucking rights. They were fucking animals, savages, and psychopaths on the loose. They had a thirst that would only be quenched by death.

Narma knew this job was a suicide mission. It kept him stressed the fuck out for over a couple decades, honest to God, he could not explain how he stayed sane while coping with this risk-taking day to day operation. Especially with always having his ass on the front line. His mind wasn't playing tricks with him, it was giving him his harsh reality. Something he wasn't ready for, something he could not digest so he decided to go back to thinking about Pete so he could breathe better.

"Pete are you like them too?" Narma said so he could hear himself talk as he sped down the highway. There was no one in the car with him, "Are you a Risk Taker? If you aren't then this fucking shit we signed the fuck up for is about to convert us all in to one, by fucking force and by fucking choice."

CHAPTER 19

The Feds were cheap. They used a raggedy old plane to transport prisoners. The plane was classified as a lemon. There was always a problem with the plane, it actually had grey duct tape on one of the wings and other areas outside. Transfer days constantly got delayed or postponed because of the plane breaking down or needing to be fixed. It was common for inmates to have to be returned to the same institution because something wasn't working right.

Today the plane was high among the clouds, only two hours behind schedule due to engine problems. Every time the plane transports it would be filled to capacity. There was a twelve-officer crew, two served as pilots, three had medical degrees, and there wasn't anything special about the other seven aboard - they were just regular staff members. A total of ten of them dressed the prisoners out, as well as draped and dripped the people out in shining shackles and chains. The troublemakers and high-profile people had a custom made piece of jewelry to go along with their monkey suit, it was called, "THE BLACK BOX", an inmate designed and was rewarded a handsome fifty dollars, for his invention.

Once the plane reaches its destination, there would be various other vehicles waiting to pick up or drop off prisoners.

Once the trade was made the plane was back in the air to finish off the eight hours of transporting for the day.

Every blue moon everything would go according to schedule. Today wasn't a historic day. The pilots did not have to assault the wheels for landing. The raggedy ass plane came to a successful stop and all twelve of the plane's staff armed themselves with vests and weapons of their choice. Here they all had more than one role to play but was only getting one check.

The two pilots were first to exit the plane. The three medical staff rushed off to unload the plastic crates loaded with medication. There's always going to be herds of officers holding secret meetings on both sides of the plane, the prisoners will take their baby steps between them going and coming. No prisoners are allowed on or off the plane until their name has been called. Once they are cleared through verification by stating their name, prison number, and date of birth, they will board their next transport vehicle bus, van, or car.

Meanwhile, from a half a mile away, on top of a hill Risgo, Gangsta Slim, and Mr. Kibble sat in the patrol car. They watched through their binoculars as the Federal Agents called the inmates names and escorted them off of the airplane.

Risgo and Gangsta had previously watched this episode three times. Once a week they witnessed this same routine and today it went accordingly, nothing different.

"How many is out there?" Mr. Kibble asked, because every time he looked through his binoculars he became more nervous and was about to have a panic attack.

"A few dozen," Risgo answered knowing Mr. Kibble's

question was how many law enforcement officers were present.

"There's nothing to worry about," Gangsta Slim said. "Mr. Kibble everything is going to work as planned," he reassured Mr. Kibble to calm him down. Gangsta Slim knew everything he said, Kibble viewed it as law. "Mr. Kibble Sir, this is a catwalk, we've been through shit a lot more complicated than this," he added for good measure.

"And y'all came out like a rose." Risgo provided assistance for Gangsta Slim with calming the genius' nerves.

Mr. Kibble was wise enough to know Gangsta Slim was referring to their first mission, when they were successful with stealing the missiles off the military base while under the heaviest security.

"That's why I call you my hero," Mr. Kibble said while coming back to reality from revisiting the past.

"Genius, you too much of a thinker," Gangsta Slim began, "all of them put together can't outthink you," Gangsta Slim's strong words were like a shot of whisky for Mr. Kibble.

The fear abandoned his body as he remembered that the ability to think was the greatest asset that God could have ever given a human being.

"So, what we going to do, G.?"

"We are going to follow through with our plan."

"You ready Mr. Kibble?" Risgo asked.

"I'm going to ride with G until the wheels fall off," Mr. Kibble said as he laid back into seat of the police car.

Risgo began talking into his walky-talky letting the Maiseyon's army know they were in motion to execute plan A. They were more than ready to bring World War III, and IV if needed- kill or be killed was their way of life. These guys weren't new to it, but true to it. They breathed and lived for shit like this. That's why they liked Gangsta Slim and his family because they had this way of life in common, trained to go day to day activity.

"I love this shit," Risgo heard one of the Mexicans whisper in the background of one of the commander's walky-talky.

"Kill yaself," another silly Mexican fired off, also getting hyped and ready to spill the pigs' blood.

The Maiseyon had two hundred heavily armed guys there to aid and assist. They had the plane and transport vehicles surrounded like Indians as they spread out incognito. They could have slaughtered all the agents before they realized what was happening, but they had to go through Gangsta Slim's plan because The Maiseyon made him the lead hunter. Some of the Mexicans secretly prayed for something to go wrong so they could get the green light to give the law Enforcers a first-class ticket to hell. Also, there was another addition of three hundred more of the Maiseyon's soldiers within a two-mile radius. The Maiseyon took no deadly measures- they breed killers.

"We going in," Risgo alerted as he put the patrol cruiser in gear and put the vehicle in motion.

"We got y'all's back amigo, one hundred percent. We going to war for y'all and with y'all," The Mexican stamped.

"That's what the fucks up," Risgo said.

Gangsta Slim sat in the passenger seat and put on his police shades and police hat. He wasn't scared nor nervous, he stopped that when he was fourteen years old. Instead, he was thirsty for adventure. This danger always attracted him. Now him and Risgo were considered certified veterans. They feared the only two things that Uncle Louta feared, God and what they would do to a muthafucka.

"Mr. Kibble, this nothing to a giant," Risgo said, using the phase he heard Gangsta Slim use on him.

"OK, Giant," Mr. Kibble replied.

"Mr. Kibble, this ya world," Gangsta Slim said, "I'm just a squirrel in it."

"OK, Squirrel," Mr. Kibble replied as he began to focus on the task that stood before him, because being around a lot of people always made him feel uncomfortable. Gangsta Slim always encouraged him to find his comfort zone deep within self and go there. stay there because this was a very important mission. Mr. Kibble did not want to let Gangsta Slim down and most important he did not want to fail self.

CHAPTER 20

2:30 A.M.

Five truckloads of agents turned down Uncle Louta's mile long driveway. After a quarter of a mile Narma pulled over, he was leading the pack and needed to make sure all agents under him knew how he ran his show. The dusty dirty dirt road kicked dust up kicked dust up everywhere. They had to let the dust settle and clear up before they all exited their vehicles. They rode four men deep and all anticipated in playing their magical role intaking Uncle Louta down. For some strange reason, their Chief of Bureau classified Uncle Louta as an old gangster. When it was pretty much clear and known all around the world that the government was the real gangsters the certified OGs. Their chief had finally come to the conclusion that now was the best time ever to take Louta Williams down, as well as to make history off of him. So, their law abiding citizens would not try to follow in the bad guys footsteps.

Pete climbed out of the back seat of Narma and Reese's four door SUV. He wanted to feed his lungs. As he was firing up the cigar, the other truck doors began to open. One of the agents started a frivolous conversation about how filthy the dirt road had dirtied up his truck.

"That will give you something to do tomorrow," one of his passengers popped off, "that way you'll be working the body instead of your jaws." He made the funny statement because this guy always complained about something and if it wasn't one thing it was another.

"Guys, Guys, Guys," Narma said as he began walking towards the two guys, "I need all of you guys full attention. I know in the last couple meetings we talked about our suspect here and there, but still, even I don't know what to expect coming from this guy. He is full of surprises and very very unpredictable. Louta is extremely dangerous. Our goal is to take him alive. But before I jeopardize one of you guys life, I'll say we'll let our director stand over him and look down at his dead body. My men's lives are very valuable to me."

The guys unprofessional comments began to surface, "I'll knock his ass off," one agent said, hyping himself up, "OOooohuoo Baby," he hollered.

"I'll kill the son-a-bitch"

"We ain't gotta worried bout getting judged by twelve"

"License to kill, baby," he also hollered, "hhuoo."

"I ain't tryin get carried by six."

Narma stood there allowing them to get all the bullshit out of their system before he took back over the show He always gave his crew fifteen good minutes of fun. If his crew members had to talk crazy before missions to psych themselves up, then so be it.

"I'm the number one sniper throughout our district," the guy said, loud and proud.

"How long you been a sniper?" Reese asked.

"Six years."

"We up against a guy who has been a snipper for no less than five decades." Narma further explained, "He used to train agents back in the day before he turned full-fledged into his criminal ways. He used to fight for his country. They wanted him to become a secret service agent, but he declined. Louta Williams is not your ordinary guy even though he's in his mid-70's."

The guys put all of their bullshit to the side and allowed Narma to talk without any more interruptions. The more they learned about their man the better. Besides Narma's been around, he wasn't their top rank agent because of his age, but because of his knowledge.

Reese thought to himself, if him, Narma, and Pete wasn't careful their crew would mess around and get themselves killed and them as well. Out of the sixteen agents the oldest one was only thirty-two years old.

"Reese, you have anything you feel you need to share?" Narma asked as he tried to turn the floor over to Reese, especially since he noticed him giving something a great deal of thought.

"No, you're doing a great job."

"Pete?" Narma asked giving Pete the chance to elaborate on anything he felt needed or thought that should be said.

"I think you said it all," Pete replied and continued giving his cigar hell.

"Everyone get in gear," Narma instructed.

"Boss, we twenty deep," one of the young agents addressed Narma and paused to take a spit, to free his mouth from his dip "we should take this old man down with ease."

"We dealing with a man with six decades of experience," Pete spoke for Narma as he held up six fingers making sure the young guy could hear and see the number six.

"Louta Williams has six senses, which is totally one more than us. You all know what the number six represents?" Pete paused, looking around, he wanted one of them to answer.

"The beast," Reese spitted out.

"Correct," Pete applauded.

"The man is a cold-hearted animal," Narma stated and stopped, truly he wanted to say more, but decided it would be best to keep it to himself.

Uncle Louta was capable of knocking at least half of their men off because they would make the tender mistake of underestimating him by thinking they are quicker or smarter than the old man. That is why Narma pointed out and poured out facts and used Reese and Pete to assist him with waking up their team because they were sleeping on the old owl. Narma, Pete, and Reese talked among themselves as their team got suited and booted.

"I dreaded this day would come," Pete spit through clenched teeth.

"How you guys think we gonna come out?" Narma seriously asked.

"Hopefully, we'll be successful," Reese said with wishfully thinking.

"This mission will be like no other mission," Pete said in between taking puffs from his cigar. His eyes were glossed over as he talked, he started off into space, "Difficult. Here we have to bring some ass in order to get some ass."

"Louta is more damn dangerous than a clan of terrorists by his got damn self," Reese stated and surely wasn't talking just because he had a mouth.

"Then he will be a force to reckon with," one of the young agents pointed out. He was glad they shared this with him instead of among the team. It probably would have killed some of their men's spirit, but he'd want his guys to know the truth of what they were facing instead of allowing them to walk completely into the dark.. The three of them knew things concerning Uncle Louta and his vicious crew that weren't in their files. People would tell them things only if they kept it off the record.

Narma studied Pete, especially his body language. He could identify that Pete was disturbed deeply about something. Pete knew something that him and Reese did not know but desperately needed to know in order for them to better protect themselves as well as Pete's own safety.

Narma's eyes shifted back over to his team. Everyone wore all black. The guys armed themselves with weapons, vest, and masks. Some of them had night vision goggles on the top of their heads while others held theirs.

Reese kissed his silver cross and tucked it away behind his vest. He cut his eyes over to Narma to see if he was ready to give the command.

"One truck load will follow us; we'll drive up to his house and the rest of you will take the woods. Guys be careful and I want y'all to know, sometimes when it comes to dealing with this guy, I don't know what to expect. I don't know what we are walking into and today we all are walking blind," Narma said, being completely honest with his men and himself as well.

CHAPTER 21

As Risgo guided the vehicle closer and closer the more nervous Mr. Kibble became. He was on perfect timing; the agents had secured the last prisoner onto his rightful transport carrier. Now the agents stood around engaging in small talk and wasting time because they were getting a pretty penny for being a glorified babysitter. They got paid for every second, minute, and hour, so the bullshit conversations helped to waste time and burn the clock.

Once Risgo reached a half mile, some of the agents gave him their full attention, but not in a panicked way. They did not see him as a threat, especially since he was behind the wheel of a police car. The head man in charge of security walked away from the pack. He wanted to know what these two officers wanted and why they were running late. He held out his right hand instructing Risgo to bring the car to a halt and kill the engine. As soon as Risgo came in compliance the security guy twisted his wrist and motioned for them to exit the vehicle and come forward.

"I got my eye on everything cuz," Risgo said.

"Alright," Gangsta Slim mumbled as he abandoned the passenger seat. Upon stepping out the vehicle, he did not close the door all the way. The security frowned as he watched Gangsta Slim making his way towards him. Gangsta Slim wore a police uniform, shades, and shiny black shoes. Once he reached six feet, the security guy asked the important question, "Why are you here?"

Gangsta Slim held up his right hand, which clearly indicated shut the fuck up and listen. "I'm on a top-secret mission and you can be a part of this, only if you want to. If you're not interested, I'm going to need you to keep this shit strictly between you and me because it'll be both of our asses and heads on the line."

The security guy wanted to snap because he didn't like for blacks to feel or be more important than himself, but his curiosity got the best of him. He pushed his pride to the side and said, "Shoot, I'm listening and this here shit better be good." as he looked at Gangsta Slim's name tag, which read G. Williams, Gangsta Slim's real name which he would not know if it was true or false.

"In my back seat I have the scientist who murdered his four scientist partners and stole the six nuclear warhead missiles. There is a two million dollar reward out for this guy, you follow me?"

"I'm listening Williams."

"We can split that shit fifty-fifty," Gangsta Slim paused. He had the head security agent's full attention as he removed his phone off of his belt clip, "You should know all about this guy who I'm talking about."

"I'm familiar with him," the head agent guy lied, as well as felt ashamed and embarrassed that he wasn't accustomed to Gangsta Slim allegations, which he was telling him the honest truth, without being under oath concerning Mr. Kibble.

Gangsta Slim tapped on his phone and a moment later a picture of Yan Kibble appeared on the screen. Gangsta Slim scrolled down showing the agent everything that fell out of his mouth was not only the God honest truth but was also public record.

The agent's heart was beating faster than Mr. Kibble's. Here he was fifty-six years old and has never liked a black man, because of his color. Now he wanted to hug and kiss Gangsta

Slim because Slim was giving him the beautiful and blissful opportunity to fulfill his dream of becoming a millionaire. The agent wanted to leap for joy, knowing the sun only shines on the dog's ass once.

Once in a lifetime opportunity knocks. He smiled because his secret agenda was to steal all of Gangsta Slim's credit by bring Yan Kibble to justice so that he'll be America's number one hero.

"Sir, let me see your phone, so I can call my director and get you the top security clearance you need." Gangsta Slim asked as he held out his right hand and to his surprise the agent handed it over.

Gangsta Slim immediately punched in the number the Maiseyon had given him. The white man who was playing the director role was one of the militia's top assassins and was multi-talented. He specialized in assassinations and loved the thrill of the hunt and taking down his prey.

The Maiseyon was a very smart man who could give a damn about one's color, race, or creed. He wanted and needed the best of the best, plus it eliminated him from having to use his loved ones on such dangerous missions. Better them than us, the Maiseyon said often to his soldiers. As the phone was answered Gangsta Slim breathed, "Director Sir, I'm here as you planned. I have this agent standing before me," and with that Gangsta Slim passed over the phone.

"Good afternoon Sir," The agent greeted as soon as his phone touched his ear.

"May I ask who I am speaking with?"

"Agent Wright Sir," the agent spoke like a soldier was supposed to speak to a higher ranking superior.

"Wright, I take it that you already have been informed of who I am?"

"Sir, yes I have," agent Wright exhaled while sticking his chest out as if he was standing before the director.

"I sent one of my top men before you, so we can take security measures concerning Yan Kibble and bringing him to justice. I need you to give him your full assistance agent. You have my word you will get what you have coming."

"Sir, he'll get my full cooperation."

"Thank you," The so-called director replied, and the line went dead.

"So, I take it that you can get me and my prisoner on the plane," Gangsta- Slim asked.

"That would not be a problem."

Gangsta Slim motioned for Risgo to pull the car up to them, which meant that everything had went according to plan. Gangsta Slim and agent Wright walked over to the back door.

Gangsta Slim opened the door, "Mr. Kibble Sir, come on out," Agent Wright was impressed by Slim's professionalism because he gave no prisoner respect. He could care less about them having high profile cases or being the top dawg in their criminal enterprise. He still treated them all less than a human and one hundred percent like an animal.

Yan Kibble wore a thick wool orange button up jumpsuit that had county jail stamped on the back of it in large capital black letters. His wrists were cuffed, and he wore leg shackles.

"You can head on back to the county jail. We are in good hands," Gangsta Slim said as he patted on top of the police car. This gave agent Wright the impression that the driver had no clue as to what was going on.

Gangsta Slim did not so much as look back at Risgo. He just grabbed Mr. Kibble by the elbow and took baby steps with him as they headed toward the head agent.

CHAPTER 22

Uncle Louta had taught Keisword Jr. how to lay the road traps that would trigger when the weight a vehicle passed over them.

While Narma and his crew were getting prepared, so were the new Risk Takers. D.B. Jr. laid on the roof with a black blanket covering his body from head to toe. He kept his right eye focused through the scope. Uncle Louta gave him the best weapon that money could buy.

Keisword Jr. and his brothers were scattered out in the front yard with bushes on top of their heads. They used both eyes to peek through their scopes. Uncle Louta's wife was racing across the floor, pushing as fast as she could the bazooka stand that Risgo had invented. He built it thinking, someday it might come in handy. Once the stand was placed beside the bazooka cabinet, the bazooka would roll onto the stand. No muscle needed, plus the individual wouldn't have to worry about the kick back power. Risgo told Uncle Louta that he was too old to try and handle the bazooka and his nephews' little asses were too young. Now Deyarna was able to fight along with her loved ones. She waited patiently in the basement window for the gun fight to begin. Uncle Louta peeked out of his bedroom window, waiting for the enemy to walk into their own death bed.

D.B. Jr.'s gun spit twice and he whispered into his

mouthpiece, "Two down," letting the fam know two agents walked right into his scope. There were plenty more deaths guaranteed to come along like a thief in the night.

The death toll increased by two more notches because Keisword Jr. and his baby brothers got a man a piece. The agents did not know what had hit them.

Uncle Louta gave the boys instructions- under no circumstance were they to move. Stay put no matter what because the enemy had to cross their path in order to get to him. Uncle Louta made himself the decoy since he was the one they were after.

The agents were able to see nothing other than one another falling dead as they worked their way through the woods. Their night vision goggles, and vest were useless. They were being shot in the eyes, neck, and head. They wanted to retreat, tuck their tails in and make a run for it. They realized they were fighting a losing battle. They were in a no-win situation, fighting against snipers they could not see..

"They knew we were coming," one of the agents cried out.

"I can't see them," another agent said, but he could have saved his breath.

"None of us can," confirmed another agent.

"They are in and on the ground," the snipper agent reported.

"Thanks, but that's not helping us. They have the advantage on us. We can't kill what we can't see," another agent stated.

"Start firing wild rounds on the ground where you think they might be," the head agent stated.

They began firing like crazy into the woods and trees not knowing they were still a good fifty feet away. Only making themselves an easy target.

As soon as the two government trucks got within striking distance and popped up on Deyarna's computer screen, she zeroed in as Risgo showed her. Once the code green produced all five circles Deyarna pushed the red button. The bazooka blasted through the window catching one of the trucks causing it to explode into scraps and sending balls of fire in the opposite direction. Uncle Louta sent four slugs into the front windshield of the other SUV but did not cause any damage. The bullet proof glass protected the agents. He mumbled, "Y'all gonna give me justice or death!"

Deyarna released another one of the bazooka' s missiles. Narma and Reese exited the truck in the nick of time before it made contact and exploded. As the truck flipped over backwards, Narma and Reese stepped onto Uncle Louta's front yard a few feet away from his nephew's and forced him to exit the house. He was bare foot and shirtless. Uncle Louta wore a pair of cut off blue jeans and carried a super light rifle. He burst through the screen door ready to kill whoever was in sight. As he looked through his scope, finger on the trigger, two agents fired at him only missing by a couple inches. Uncle Louta made sure they did not get a second chance. He shot one after the other in the face. Anytime he pulled the trigger, it was for a kill shot.

One of the agents was a couple feet away from Keiwon. Uncle Louta hollered towards him and the agent swung his M-16 around to shoot Uncle Louta until his body turned to fish food. Keiray burst up out of the ground, screaming and hollering as he was racing towards the agent, which spooked the agent to death. D.B. Jr released a bullet catching the agent in the forehead. The other four agents in the woods became trigger happy as they became incognito. They laid on the ground trying to play the waiting game as well, but Deyarna brought their copy-cat idea to an end by sending one of the bazooka's missiles their way. She put them out of their misery by blowing them into pieces and sparking a serious forest fire.

The air was foggy with dirt, dust, and smoke. Narma had Uncle Louta in his scope, "you barefoot vigilant," he whispered with his finger on the trigger. Narma blinked one time too many. When he looked through his scope again, his and Uncle Louta's scope were eye to eye. He panicked while squeezing off a round.

Uncle Louta released two. The first bullet knocked Narma's

bullet out of the air. The second one hit him in the neck. Reese witnessed the whole scene. He had laid face down in the grass playing dead. Since he wasn't able to go hard, he had to do the next best thing and that was to play smart.

As Uncle Louta was backing into his front door, Pete was walking across his living room. Pete also got smart by telling Narma to stop the truck and let him get out. He took the woods opposite side of the other agents and was successful with breaking into the back of Uncle Louta's house.

He knocked Deyarna unconscious with the butt of his pistol. She laid in a huge puddle of her own blood.

POW! POW! Pete's two shots echoed through the house as he shot Uncle Louta twice in the side. While Uncle Louta was falling Pete snatched the rifle out of his hand.

"Ooh," Uncle Louta managed to exhale after hitting the floor hard. He laid on his back.

Pete stood over Uncle Louta smiling, "Tell me that really did not hurt?"

"Which ones, the shots or the fall?" Uncle Louta asked as he looked into Pete's eyes clearly letting him know there wasn't any fear in him.

"The fall of course," Pete answered.

"You always been my guardian angel, but this time you came as the Grimm-Reaper," Uncle Louta groaned out.

Pete had killed many people for Uncle Louta and informed him every time the law enforcers was on to him or Gangsta Slim's trail. If he did not report to Uncle Louta that Toshiba was sexing that agent, they all would be buried alive in prison or in the ground with a tombstone over their heads.

"Louta, all I have done for you and you still would not let me go free. You old son-of-bitch, you the fucking devil."

Uncle Louta smiled back up at Pete, "You fucking right! I might be the devil but there's one thing you forgot."

"What's that?" Pete asked.

"I have demons that guard me."

Pete was a tad bit too slow as he finally saw D.B. Jr's

shadow on the living room wall. D.B. Jr. fired one shot knocking a chunk out of Pete's head. His dead body beat the empty shell case to the floor.

"Thank you, son," Uncle Louta said, now he could breathe better.

"That's how I was able to repay you for all of your tutor training."

"Help me sit up." Uncle Louta asked.

"You been hit Unk, we gotta get you to a doctor."

"Shit, we gotta get the hell out of here, would be more like it," Uncle Louta said and asked for his rifle.

Once D.B. Jr. handed it to him, Uncle Louta politely scooped himself over to Pete's already dead body and put the barrel into his mouth and pulled the trigger, "My snitch, I need for you to have a fucking closed casket."

Keisword Jr., Keiwon, and Keiray raced into the living room, "Unk, you ok?" Keisword Jr asked.

"Other than the two souvenirs on my side. I'm alright. Now go find my beautiful wife, so we can take our escape route out of here."

"Unk, you think I shoot good," D.B. Jr. asked.

"You the best sniper in the whole wide world."

D.B. Jr. looked from Keiwon to Keiray, "Unk, they are too. I couldn't have done it without them,"

"Son, you right," Uncle Louta said and waived them all to him. They all hugged him together. His wound pain was replaced by love. "All you guys are the best. I don't know what I would've done without you guys. Y'all give an old man like me the spirit to continue to wake up in the morning."

"Unk, what my daddy was like?" D.B. Jr. asked, because all he ever heard his daddy was a cold-hearted killer or an animal.

Uncle Louta rubbed D.B. Jr.'s head and said, "He was a Williams, just like you."

D.B. Jr cocked his head sideways and looked confused, "Unk, the agent that was asking me a lot of questions said that all of the Williams is animals."

"What do you think?" Uncle Louta asked.

Keisword Jr., D.B. Jr, Keiwon, and Keiray all answered his question by growling.

CHAPTER 23

Wright and Gangsta Slim escorted Mr. Kibble towards the group of agents.

The agent looked down to his clipboard, "We have no one late," he said as he looked in Wright's direction.

Wright did his famous hand motion. First, he produced an open palm facing up, indicating the agent to hold that thought. Then he twisted his wrist and waived the agent over to them so they could speak in private. Wright took a couple steps away from Mr. Kibble and Gangsta Slim. He wanted his coworker to feel free to voice his opinion, but it wasn't going to overrule his decision because his mind was already made up.

"What is this?" He asked Wright, as the color in his face began to fade.

"This is something bigger than me and you."

The agent looked at him crazy, "Wright, that's not telling me anything."

"I got a call from the Director. He said for these two people to board our plane. "

"I would need to hear the Director give that order."

Wright threw that same palm into his face, "You saying you

don't trust me? You don't trust the instructions I passed down to you?"

"I'm saying it would be more approvable, a little more satisfactory. That's all I'm saying."

"What is my job title?"

"You the Head of Security, but---."

Wright cut his sentence off in midair, "I cannot explain due to security measures. The higher-ups and my job will not allow me to be in a breach of security."

"Who are those two guys?" He still asked, disregarding what Wright had just said.

"I'm not able to answer any of your questions, at least not at the moment. Once all this is over, you have my word, you will be the first person to interview me and to get my autograph."

"Wright, if this shit doesn't go well, please know that I will not allow myself and the crew to go down with you like the fucking Titanic. All I'm saying is be 21 about everything."

"You have my word," Wright said, extending his right hand, the agent stumbled and pouted as he walked away, leaving Wright's right-hand hanging. Wright waved Gangsta Slim and Mr. Kibble over, "everything is dandy and beautiful," Wright said.

"I never rode a plane," Mr. Kibble admitted.

"It's like riding a bike," Wright predicted.

."I never rode a bike," Mr. Kibble admitted again.

"You ever fired a gun?" Wright asked, thinking about the other scientist that they claimed Mr. Kibble murdered in cold blood.

"Nooo," Mr. Kibble replied.

"Then what have you done?" Wright asked as he took the

stairs to the plane behind Mr. Kibble one by one.

"Worked in labs practically all of my life." Mr. Kibble said almost out of breath. "Straight out of high school. A normal life would be foreign to me and my way of life you normal people would think would be foreign as well."

"The only thing I like foreign is my women and my vehicles," Wright said as he allowed Mr. Kibble to entertain him.

Actually, he thought Mr. Kibble's ill formed looking ass would do good in a circus. The people would pay a fortune to come and see his ugly short super intelligent ass.

Upon boarding the plane, Gangsta Slim had to hand over his bullets, pistol, loose pocket change, and keys. He was allowed to keep his phone. As they were taking baby steps down the aisle of the plane, Gangsta Slim stressed the importance why he needed to be seated beside Mr. Kibble and the importance that he watch his hands at all times.

"If he so much as stretches his muscles, I'm watching. When he pisses and shits, I'm watching. I keep his lil' hands in plain view at all times," Gangsta Slim said.

"You a watching ass," Wright said, smiling, "Shit, better you than me. But that is what comes with the territory of being a glorified babysitter.

Within 45 minutes of the flight, 36 and counting popped up on Gangsta Slim's touch screen, which clearly told him he had 30 minutes to complete his mission and the clock was ticking.

He looked over to Mr. Kibble as they sat side by side, "How long will it take you to work your magic?" Gangsta Slim whispered to him.

"Give or take 6 to 8 minutes."

Gangsta Slim placed his phone into Mr. Kibble's small palms, "You have 7 minutes, tops."

"I'll beat the deadline in that case," Mr. Kibble said as his fingers began to tap and dance away on the touch screen. It wouldn't take long because he knew beforehand what had to be done, besides this was his line of work.

Gangsta Slim set his stopwatch on 30 minutes. He disregarded the extra 6 minutes because that was the extra minutes they added to put insurance on themselves. He actually counted down on Mr. Kibble and to his surprise Mr. Kibble beat the buzzer by a whole minute. He handed Gangsta Slim back his phone, "We good."

"We good?" Gangsta Slim repeated.

"Yes, sir."

Gangsta Slim reached over and popped open Mr. Kibble's cuffs and handed him the key, so he could remove his own leg shackles. Gangsta Slim stood to make his announcement because he wanted to see the expression of the agent's faces, "Ladies and Gentlemen, may I please have your attention?"

Agent Wright gave him a daring look. Gangsta Slim put Wright's same motion on him by throwing a palm up to keep him from speaking.

"Agent Wright, me and my people have full control of this plane. We are not trying to high-jack your plane, but if you all don't meet our demands, we'll crash this bitch. Yes, killing all of you muthafuckas."

"How we know you have our plane under control?" One of the women agents asked in a panicked voice.

Gangsta Slim handed his phone pack to Mr. Kibble, "Turn the plane slightly to the right until I tell you to stop."

Mr. Kibble tilted the phone in his left hand, as he used his right trigger finger to draw a line across the screen. The plane moved to the right until Slim instructed Kibble to stop. The agents and prisoners oohed and awed as they feared for their life as well as safety.

"Now do the other side."

Mr. Kibble tipped the other side as well confirming he was their pilot. One of the actual pilot's voice came over the loudspeaker confessing he was having technical difficulty and asked that everyone please remain in their seats.

"Do you have complete control of this plane?" Wright asked. The pilot remained silent, so Wright repeated himself, "Agent, do you have complete control of our plane. Yes or No?"

"I'm afraid not," the pilot admitted.

"We gonna die."

"Oh my God, they going to kill us."

"What do these villains want from us?"

Some of the agents took turns exercising their voices but no one addressed their concerns to Gangsta Slim. Since Wright brought him aboard, they all slurred at him for answers. So, he asked, "why are you here?"

"You have a package and I'm the repo man. Once I get what I came for you have my word, I'll be completely out of your hair."

"What fucking package?" Wright asked through closed teeth.

If he would have been able to wrap his large hands around Gangsta Slim's neck he would have strangled him to death.

Gangsta Slim's eyes never left Wright's as he talked,

"Segre?"

Gangsta Slim called out and got no answer. Which led him to believe he was pronouncing the name wrong. He told himself that he still should be close to it.

"Si, Si, Senor, Si," Segre replied, (Yes, Yes sir, yes.)

"Stand so I can see you," Slim demanded.

Another Mexican close by him translated the sentence to him and told Gangsta Slim what Segre was trying to say.

"Mr. Kibble Sir?"

"Yes, G."

"Open the plane door, we came through."

Within seconds the door opened, and the air rushed in rearranging things that were to light in the ass. Gangsta Slim pointed to the female agent that was the closest to Segre, "Take all of y'all's jewelry off him."

The woman looked over to Wright and thought now this muthafucka is about to get me caught up in his bullshit. Gangsta Slim picked up on her body language. He was on the clock; time was steadily ticking away, so he reconstructed his order and directed it straight at Wright. "Wright, would you please do the honor and free the important man of all those restraints."

"'Do I have a choice?" Wright asked, being sarcastic.

"The choice is completely up to you. But if you don't, I promise you, I will send this whole fucking plane to the bottom of the ocean." Gangsta Slim promised. "And Wright, that's a promise, not a threat by the way."

Wright completed the task that was asked of him.

Gangsta Slim commanded Mr. Kibble to go over and stand beside Segre. Gangsta Slim thought Segre was too young and small to have six bodies underneath his belt. He was almost five feet flat and did not weigh a hundred pounds. Serge stared at one of the agents. He wanted to kill the man for not giving him enough to eat.

"Wright, me and my two men going to jump off this plane. Please for the people on this plane sake don't try any funny business."

"How I know you won't still crash us?" Wright asked.

"You don't, you just have to trust me on that one."

"Do I have a choice?"

"Nah, not for real," Slim replied while securing his jumping equipment and nodding at Kibble to make sure he did the same.

"I have your word, if me and my men allow y'all to jump ship you will not bury us in the bottom of the ocean?" Wright reworded his question.

"I don't believe in double jeopardy…. punishing the people for their sins because I'm a sinner myself." Soon as Gangsta Slim finished his sentence, his watch alarm went off, alerting him it was time to jump. He walked over to Mr. Kibble and Serge, "We have to jump now," they followed him to the door, "Jump Mr. Kibble."

Serge did not need any instructions. He hopped off the plane because he would rather be dead than to be in prison. It took all of the will power Wright possessed in his body not to run to the door and holler at Gangsta Slim, you black muthafucka. Instead, he stayed, glued to his seat revisiting the moment. All of the clues stood out clear as day, but he could not see them because he was blinded by his own damn greed. Wright pushed send on his phone to the number G. Williams claimed to be the Director's. What happened, just what he thought would happen, "this number is out of service." the automated service said.

***

Risgo watched the water from a distance through his binoculars. The alligators and crocodiles had gotten some of the floating packages off top of the water and had taken them to the bottom and buried them.

"That's good," he announced, "Things are working with us and not against us." Risgo reported to his baby army. The Maiseyon had given him 75 men.

The soldiers were faithful and under his control. Once Risgo's watch alarm went off he held up his right hand so everyone who needed to see it could see it. As soon as Risgo dropped his hand to his side the explosions began. They went off for a good ten minutes straight. The reptile's bodies replaced the floating packages as they floated on top of the water. Some were even thrown were thrown onto the dry land.

Risgo took another look into his binoculars. There wasn't a live creature in sight, "we should be good guys, but to be on the safe side, I need about fifteen of you to walk into the water until it comes up to your waist." They followed suit with their M-16's ready to make any other alligator or crocodile lunch, dinner, and supper or clothing and shoe material. The water was calm and a good thing Risgo followed his first mind because at least a dozen of the reptiles played possum or buried themselves in at the bottom.

They came out for the enemies and attacked nine soldiers before they were also cut to pieces from the array of bullets.

Risgo commanded them to put more packages of explosives into the water. He would rather be safe than sorry.

"How many packages?"

"Same number," Risgo said, while looking at this watch, "Let's hurry people, we are expecting our real packages in 11 minutes."

The Mexicans worked together like ants. They raced back and forth, speaking in nothing but Spanish. Risgo did not give a fuck about him not understanding a damn thing. They were raising hell among themselves. He was a hundred percent positive they were with him and not against him.

"Everything in place," a soldier told him. "Blow that muthafucka."

The explosions took their toll and this time everything was copasetic. Risgo told all of the soldiers to walk into the water waist deep. He did the same and they all played Russian roulette knowing the 20ft long reptiles promised to give them a quick and painless death by biting and snapping their bodies in two. One bite would have half of their body gone.

"You know men, there's two kinds of people in this world," Risgo said.

"What kind is that American man?" The soldier asked while smiling because he liked to talk shit as well as listen to others talk shit.

Risgo continued to look towards the sky, "The ones who go out and make shit happen and the ones who sit back and wait on shit to fall out of the sky."

"So, which one are you?"

"Both," Risgo replied as their package came into sight.

Another Mexican started singing, "Dum-Dum-Dumdum,"

as if there was a couple getting ready to walk down the aisle.

"You're the next contestant on the Price is Right. Come on down," another Mexican said in his Bob Barker voice.

They were really ready to clown, party, drink, smoke weed, and celebrate as they laid eyes on Gangsta Slim, Mr. Kibble, and their comrade Segre flying through the air. Before they could hit the water 20 soldiers threw down their weapons and began swimming under the water.

"'One."

"Two."

"Three."

One of the soldiers counted off with pride as Gangsta Slim, Mr. Kibble, and Segre's small bodies hit the water hard. All three were headed straight to the bottom quick, fast, and in a hurry, but were intercepted by the soldiers. They caught them and swam to the top of the water. Gangsta Slim and Mr. Kibble said they could swim, so they were allowed to do so, but on the other hand they had fun with Segre. They tossed his ass around to one another until all 19 of them touched him. They were happy to see him and he was happier to be back amongst them.

Once Gangsta Slim made it over to Risgo's presence, Risgo did not hesitate to give him the update concerning Uncle Louta and their nephews.

"They had come to arrest Unk, but remember how he used to set all of them traps in the woods and on the dirt road? That's how he was able to be a step ahead of them. They walked straight into the ambush."

"Shit," Gangsta Slim cussed, it hurt him to his heart that he wasn't able to be there to give assistance when his presence was desperately needed.

"They all safe, Unk got hit twice in the side. Deyarna got a few stitches to the head, but they are both under the doctor's care. The doctor says they need a few days of rest. The Maiseyon gave me his word that once Unk finished getting his proper rest he'll have his men to bring them through the tunnel."

"The underground tunnel that runs from the United States to Mexico?" Gangsta Slim asked. As he stood there soaking and wet his drenched clothes added another ten to twenty pounds of weight on him.

"Yes, now come on so we can get you a set of dry clothes."

Risgo led Gangsta Slim to the truck where he found pants, shirts, and black boots. Risgo always stayed prepared. Some of the Mexicans had skinned a reptile tail here and there, as well as had cut the meat into cube shape sizes. They ate them one by one.

"Raw Gator?" Gangsta Slim asked.

"Sushi is raw fish," Risgo corrected. "Same shit, they both live in the water.

"Gator steak, my friend," another Mexican said. "They both good to build up nature," he paused, putting both hands on his small waist as he demonstrated by hunching the air, "makes you fucky-fucky long time."

Gangsta Slim and Risgo laughed. So did the other Mexicans. But deep down in their hearts, they knew their brother was talking from experience and giving out nothing but the absolute truth, even though he stayed joking.

"Please give me some of that?" Mr. Kibble said, "and when you think I've eaten enough please get me one of those beautiful Sin-ya-Rentals."

"As you wish."

Segre walked over with his personal interpreter. He looked at Gangsta Slim as he spoke in Spanish. His interpreter translated it and repeated his words in English.

"Sir, I would like to thank you for rescuing me. You put your life on the line for me. From this day forward, I look at you and the little guy as my brothers. I will go to war on the front line with you guys any day." Segre hugged Gangsta Slim and Mr. Kibble and shook both of their hands.

Mexican soldiers started bringing forth crate after crate of bottles of beer and wine. Once everyone had a bottle of their choice he said, "I like to make a toast, a toast to the Risk Takers," they held their bottles up into the air and said in a unison, "To the Risk Takers."

Epilogue

Narma was in critical condition for four days. He spent another two inches away from his deathbed and on the seventh day, God intervened. Proving to the doctors that he was still in the blessing business. God wasn't finished with Narma yet.

Narma and Reese retired, but Narma did not like throwing in the towel. In his free time, he counseled the troubled youth. He wanted them to see what God had in store for them before they began to lean on their own understanding. He did not want to sit back and watch them throw away their future, by becoming the bad guy because when it all is said and done, crime don't pay…it is a waste of time and energy. The world does not need any more killers or criminals and there is a shortage of real O.G.'s coming forward to tell the young generation the truth, the whole truth, and the Godly truth! As well as to teach them the law of the land. If one can't help a man, then one shouldn't seek to harm a man.

Reese finally found his soulmate. He keeps her barefoot and pregnant. Since his race was dying out like dinosaurs and getting swallowed up by jaws. Reese's seeds would rebuild the nation, bring forth generation after generation. His family promised to join Narma's bandwagon to decrease the death toll numbers and the unnecessary high rate of incarceration.

Through the strong influence of Uncle Louta, they all decided to settle down and live life in the motherland. Africa keeps the Williams family veins calm, but when they need their thirst quenched, they do their dirt in other countries. Uncle did not want them to shit were they lay their heads. He told all the women they had to bear fruits, bring forth life, which was their duty to God. His wife had three children even though Uncle Louta was in his 80's. He was the true definition that Gangstas don't die, they only multiply.

COMING SOON

ORDER FORM
Make **Money Orders** PayableTo:
KBA Publications
PO BOX 2863
Phenix City, AL 36868

QTY	KBA Publications Available	Price
	A Daughter's Cry	$15
	Career Criminal	$15
	Ridaz – Part II of Career Criminal	$15
	Trans-4-ma-tion Part I	$15
	Trans-4-ma-tion Part II	$15
	Atl's Finest Part 1	$15
	Atl's Finest Part II	$15
	Port City Playaz	$15
	Opportunist Part I	$15
	Opportunist Part II	$15

Ship To:

Name: _________________________________

Address: _______________________________

City: ___________________ State: _______ Zip: _______

For Shipping and Handling: Add $3.75 for 1st Book. Add $1.75 for each additional book. All books are also available on Amazon and Kindle. All titles coming soon, also can be pre-ordered.